Old One-Toe

MICHEL-AIMÉ BAUDOUY

Old One-Toe

Illustrated by Johannes Troyer

TRANSLATED FROM THE FRENCH BY MARIE PONSOT

HARCOURT, BRACE & WORLD, INC., NEW YORK

c.11.61

Originally published in France under the title
Le Seigneur des Hautes Buttes

Library of Congress Catalog Card Number: 59-10944

Printed in the United States of America

Old One-Toe

I

The red-haired girl turned over the sheet of note paper, took a deep breath, and began to write again.

"And the forest is enormous. It's just full of trees. Animals too. But no lions and no cocodriles. Tatie's house is off to the side of the forest which is good because it is sunny. Also there is food for Tatie's chickens. Today Tatie drove the station wagon to Fontenay and we are minding the house and everything. Piet's gone fishing with Lina. Tatie took Mascot with her."

A voice called through the window, "Hurry up, Genevieve! Every time it's your turn to write, you take all day." Then the boy the voice belonged to climbed in over the sill and bent over his sister's shoulder. "Hey, look how you spelled crocodiles! Mom will die laughing when she sees that. But leave it and come on. Just stick in 'love and kisses,' and you're done."

Genevieve frowned, and reread her letter. It looked very short. With a little tug of homesickness, she wrote, "We miss you so much. Everything's fine. Love and kisses. Genevieve."

"At last! Now come on. Lina can do the envelope later. Let's go."

They ran out of the house down the path that led to the brook. Lina waved at them to be quiet. She made a sign with her hands far apart and hissed, "It's that big. It's a trout, a huge one. Look, he's almost caught it."

Piet was leaning against a tree trunk, quiet and intent. He had his rod tight against his hip, and his line disappeared into a sunlit patch of water. Under the water, the trout swam. It was a fine-sized fish, bronze-green, freckled with rosy dots, just covered by a shallow veil of water. For seconds at a time, its dorsal fin showed sharp above the water. They could see its fuselage-shaped shadow move below over the light-striped sand.

Piet had cast the fly just a few inches in front of the trout's nose. The trout moved in close, then in one supple twist went back to the transparent shadow of an overhanging rock.

Piet reeled in and began to get ready to cast again. He was dripping with sweat. This would be his twentieth try. If it didn't work this time, he'd wait for a luckier day. He hoped for a miracle as he cast.

But no miracle took place.

Quietly, Piet lifted his rod and reeled in the line.

"You're going to stop trying now?" asked Lina.

"Yes. There must be something or other I'm not doing right. I'll ask someone who knows about fishing. We'll catch him yet; don't you worry."

Piet was a calm boy, and very determined. He liked to think out plans in his head before trying to turn them into adventures. Even games, when Piet played them, were taken seriously. Lina had to respect his way of doing things. She was younger than he, though two inches taller and much more inventive. He was adored by Genevieve and Gerard, the inseparable twins.

Piet gave the brook and its trout one last threatening look and led the others back to the house.

The sound of a distant horn came from over the hill.

"The five o'clock bus!" cried Lina. "Tatie will be here before you know it."

"I don't think so," said Piet. "She won't be back before dark. She had lots of things to do in town."

"Well anyway, if it's five o'clock, we'd better feed the chickens."

Tatie's house was charming, standing white and barn-red above the brook in a circle of trees. It had once been a mill. The big mill wheel still dipped its mossy crosspieces into the water.

The rooms inside were huge, with low ceilings. On damp days they still had a vague scent of flour, mouse, and cat. The sound of water gliding under the floor of the big living room was a gentle murmur that the children soon took for granted as one of the wonders of life with Tatie. But if they looked suddenly out the window at the moving water, they seemed to see the house floating off upstream against the current while the water stood still.

When the children had first arrived, Lina had caused quite a stir. She'd no sooner come into the room than

she shrieked, covered her eyes, and cried, "The house is sailing away; the house is sailing away!"

No one could understand why she was crying, and she was crying too hard to explain. In a minute she peeked out from behind her hand, then quickly ducked back behind it. "I'm going to be sick, I'm seasick," she wailed.

The twins clapped their hands and laughed, sure that this was a new game invented by their clever sister.

Tatie, looking worried, took Lina by the shoulders and sat her down in the armchair.

Only Piet stayed calm. He did as he'd seen Lina do, looked out, saw the water, and growled, "What a nincompoop!"

"No, I'm not," Lina hiccuped. "It's moving, really it is."

"Nincompoop! It's the water that's moving. It's like being in a train and thinking the countryside is roaring past while the train sits still."

Genevieve cried, "Oh, yes, it's like the moon."

"When clouds blow over it fast and you think the moon is sailing off," added Gerard.

Tatie laughed. "You children! Lina, you made me believe the house was really going to pieces and floating away. It's so old, that's what might happen one of these days. And if ever it does, that wretched old monster will blame it all on us."

"What monster? The Commandant?"

"Of course, the Commandant. He sent me another awful registered letter just last week."

The children turned thoughtful. They already knew of Tatie's problems with the landlord, which were nothing to joke about.

"I'm going to have to pay him somehow, and pretty soon, too," said Tatie.

"You owe him the money, so of course you'll have to pay," said Piet reasonably.

They gave another minute of silence to thinking about their landlord, the cruel Commandant. Then they all sat down to a midafternoon spread of bread and butter and cheese and milk and jam and cookies. They all agreed that so much excitement makes you hungry.

Now, as they returned from their fishless fishing, Piet picked up a letter from the floor. The mailman had been by.

"It's from Mother," he said. They all crowded close, and he began to read aloud.

"Monday, 24 July. Dear children, Papa is finally out

of danger. The doctor says there is nothing more to worry about. All of his broken bones seem to be healing properly. But it will take time for him to be up and working again. I've been learning his business as fast as I can. Soon I should be able to carry on in his place until he is well again. I'm writing this at the end of a long day. It's very late, and I'm sleepy. I'm sure you are being good children, kind and obedient, for Tatie. She has a lot of work with all that poultry to raise, and I hope you are helping as much as you can."

"Speaking of helping," Lina exclaimed, "we'd better feed those chickens right away. Let's hurry and finish Mother's letter first!"

"Right," said Piet. "Tatie said to feed them at five. It's just time now."

Sunset shadows had begun to climb the hill as they left the house. They were very busy for a quarter of an hour, shaking out grain for the turkeys and chickens in the poultry yard halfway up the hill.

That done, they went on up the hill. The top was still golden with sun. They could see an infinite distance to the south, across the flatlands of the Vendée. The

world before them, a hundred shades of green, was bathed in the rose light of evening.

To the north lay the cloud-soft shapes of Mervent Forest. Its flanks burned bronze with late sun, slashed with shadows where the mists of evening had already begun to float.

The children climbed until they reached a high place overlooking the entrance to the valley where the mill lay. They had a clear view of a stretch of the road Tatie would take to come home.

Cars streamed by below them. The twins and Lina made a game of guessing the makes of the cars. Piet judged whose guess was right.

The twins defended each others' wildest guesses against all attack.

"Chevrolet!" cried Lina.

"No, Ford!" said Genevieve.

"Yes, it was a Ford '54. I saw the name written."

"You saw the name?"

"Yes, I did, I saw it. On the door!"

"What a fake! Isn't he, Piet?"

Piet said nothing, withholding judgment.

They were sitting in a patch of tall Queen Anne's lace. The twins' red heads gleamed just a little higher than the tops of the flat white flowers. The older children's hair was darker, but still russet enough to catch the sun.

The fierce pulse of three jet planes suddenly filled the air. They raced above the woods. Before the children could leap up to see, they were gone. Their trail bit off a great swathe of sky above the plain.

Gerard cried in a defiant voice, "They're Tempests!"

No one bothered to disagree. He turned to see why. Lina already was on her way down the hill. Tatie's station wagon had appeared, bumping along the road, and Lina wanted to be first to welcome her back.

Gerard ran after her, and the others followed, pell-mell.

Mascot, barking his joy in the race, soon caught up with Lina. He jumped around her, and she grabbed him as he leapt. He struggled free and ran to join Piet and the twins.

"Hi there, children," Tatie cried, as she left the car. "Where have you been?"

"Everything's fine," said Piet. "We've been feeding the chickens."

"Good," said Tatie, smiling down.

She was tall and full of life. The children loved her for her boundless energy and the imagination she put into everything. She had the gift of turning dull, everyday life into an adventure, full of surprises. Wherever she went, things seemed to take on a more brilliant color, people became fascinating, and whatever they did was delightful. Homework, even the arithmetic problems that the children couldn't bear, changed under her magic.

She'd read a problem and exclaim, "What's this all about? A man on a bicycle, going fifteen miles an hour? That reminds me of the time your mother and I took the old road to Louveciennes."

Then she'd laugh her way through the tale of a splendid race against great odds, and a glorious victory.

And then, back to the problem. "Now, about this man on a bicycle. He's doing fifteen. All right. And the man walking is doing three and a half. They're going toward each other. So let's say this white pebble is the bicyclist. The walker can be this twig. Lina, you mark out a road. Gerard, take the twig. Genevieve, take the pebble. And we'll see how it works out."

See they did, and the problem answered itself right before their eyes, with no pain at all.

When it came to describing their aunt, the children couldn't quite agree. Lina found her "really good-looking and so elegant." The twins, without ever saying so, loved her looks because her lively face reminded them delightfully of an Indian warrior chief. Only Piet voiced no opinion, which made Lina say he had no more imagination than a bread pudding.

That evening, Tatie announced, "Well, it's settled. I'll have my third incubator, latest model, next week. You'll see, things will really start popping. The poultry will increase and multiply all over the place. And next winter, we'll start ducks. Of course, I had to borrow money to the very limit. But I'm betting on the turkeys to pay it back. They're high quality stock, and the fanciest Paris butchers will buy them. The Christmas feasts of Paris's best families will pay off my new equipment."

"What about the Commandant?" asked Piet.

Tatie frowned. "That's still a problem," she admitted. "He's a hard man and wants no excuses. He demands the rent right away. If he doesn't get it, he says he'll send me notice."

"What's notice?" asked Gerard.

"Notice to get out of this mill of his if I don't pay. I think 'notice' is a word invented to bother poor people with."

"And maybe the Commandant is going to send you one?"

"Not the Commandant exactly. It's Mr. Becu, his estate agent, who handles the property for him."

"Do you know the Commandant? What does he command?"

"I don't really know, and I don't think I care. Mr. Becu calls him the Commandant. I, like a parrot, say the Commandant. Anyway he's an old meanie. But forget that now. Come to dinner."

After dinner they went for their usual walk down the road along the brook to the little bridge.

The valley was dominated on the left by the hill, and on the right by wooded slopes. It opened out into the plain from which the dim roar of threshers still resounded. Mascot romped around, barking at frogs along the brook. Sometimes he darted into the woods, but never very far in. He was too impressed by the noises coming from the mysterious shadows. Truth to tell, he didn't feel very safe there. The children encouraged him to snoop among the bushes, where he barked with fury. His young masters hoped to see him change into a real hunting dog. They'd have loved to be able to go on a hunt with him.

When they reached the road, they began their car identification game again. But Tatie said, "Oh, please do hush. Be still, and listen to the crickets."

Crickets there were. And there were quantities of other insects, making "tsetsetse" noises. There were small rock toads with their sad little piping sound. There were the groans of a tree that rubs another tree. There was the sudden flight of some creature under Mascot's nose; and the dashing rush of the dog who, unsure of the proper thing for a hunter to do, ran in and out of the hedges, hoping he'd done well. There was that great whispering stillness of woods and fields that is called silence but is not silence.

At the end of the road, there was nothing special, just empty fields and a far-off row of trees, melting into the blue of twilight. And off beyond the far fields, the lights along the road seemed to run straight to infinity in both directions.

"If we were to go off down the road," said a sober little voice.

"What would we find?" asked another voice like the first.

"Policemen," said Tatie, suddenly afraid they might one day try it. "Policemen, working hard looking to bring you back. Why? Do you want to leave? Are you tired of life at the mill?"

"Oh, no, Tatie, we love the mill," they squealed in protest.

Lina grumbled, "These little characters are idiotic."

"Give me your hands, twins," cried Tatie. "Home we go. Let's race."

Night was already spilling out of the forest to cover the lower reaches of the hill. The hilltop was still light and stood out from the sky, where the first stars shone.

Tatie glanced toward her poultry house. It looked like a big toy, forgotten halfway up the hill in the grass.

"I'm too tired to go up to see. Is everything in order there, children?"

"Yes, Tatie, everything's fine," they chorused.

II

The moon sailed big and copper-red above the hill. The little foxes stopped playing and looked toward the old log where their mother lay in shadow.

There was a sudden silence, so deep they could hear the murmur of water from the lower part of the valley.

The vixen's head snapped up. She'd fallen asleep. The silence woke her with a start. It took her a few seconds to feel in command of her kingdom once more. She blinked at the valley and the opposite slope black against the sky. Here a soft light filled the air. It showed the trees and their long shadows, the lair, the big thicket with glistening leaves, the dry clearing where the little ones were playing.

There they were, all three, the two small cubs and the sturdier, stronger one as well. Nothing had changed while she slept, except perhaps that the little ones looked even smaller and the big one even stronger. It was always like that when she woke from sleep to see them.

They were her last children. She loved all three. But the fact was that one of them was very strong and the others were not. The fact was that she was old and

tired and her milk was no longer rich. Nothing would change the facts.

The bark of a fox on the hunt echoed from afar. The sharp call woke her completely. She was hungry and yawned.

The little ones had heard, too. The hunting cry stirred their appetites. They ran toward the entrance to the lair. All there was to eat was a bit of left-over rabbit, a pheasant's carcass, and a few field mice. Not much.

The vixen came over to them. Not angrily, but firmly, she pushed Bigson aside with her paw. The weaker ones needed food more than he.

The young fox, banished, growled his resentment. It

almost seemed, for a moment, that he'd strike back. He was nearly his mother's weight, and his triangular face wore a furious expression. But he turned tail sharply and walked off with a deliberate step under the trees.

The vixen yapped a short order at him. Obediently, the sullen cub stopped and lay on the earth. He could tell which of his mother's orders demanded immediate and complete obedience. Stubborn as he was, he was still afraid of her punishments.

From a distance he watched the brothers eat. His babyhood was over. From now on, he'd have to get along on his own. He whined briefly, then cut the whine short and turned it into a yawn of irritation.

Just beside him, from under the dead leaves, a sharp cry followed his whine. He pointed his ears and drew himself up, by instinct, prodigiously still.

A mouse family was coming up out of the ground into a shaft of moonlight.

Bigson leaped, seized one on the bound, and slapped two others down with his paws.

In a wink he'd eaten them, all three. When his brothers dashed up, he was already licking his chops. Pleased with himself, he ran toward the foxhole. This time his mother let him finish the little meat that was left.

Now the white round moon was floating high in the sky. The forest was filled with a shimmering clearness. Subtle odors circulated under the trees, borne on a breeze so slight it scarcely moved the still branches.

The vixen stepped out into the clearing around the

foxhole. She moved noiselessly with a supple stride, sniffing the night air, her muzzle pointed toward the far-off sources of the subtle smells. She sat on her haunches and turned her face toward the moon. For a long minute she stared at it, then shut her eyes and gave a long howl. As she finished, the little ones shook themselves. Now their mother would have orders for them.

"Follow me, on the down-wind side." She signaled to them. "First we're going to the Old Man's House."

From the day the little ones had lost their downy coats and taken on the look of adult foxes, the vixen had hurried their education along. She knew that as soon as the season of morning fogs arrived, the forest would be overrun with howling dogs and fire-bearing men. Before then the little foxes must learn the lay of the land, its limits, its resources, and its dangers.

Day by day she taught them, starting from the foxhole, going always a little further, exercising their muscles and developing their wind in hard runs through the forest paths and in races up the pebbled slopes. The little foxes groaned. Their scratched feet were sore; low branches slapped them as they passed; the brambles tore their ears. They were hungry, they were thirsty, they were afraid, they were dead tired.

The old vixen paid no heed to their complaints and went on faster than ever.

Hunger, thirst, fear, exhaustion—they would have to know them all before leaving her as all her other children had left her. She'd forgotten them all, or rather she'd given them confidently to the forest, and they had taken their nameless places in the vast movement of trees and bushes, in the odor of damp earth. They had joined the innumerable family of lithe brigands with triangular faces, the subtle woods-runners whose red fur slips like lightning over the green shadow of the underbrush.

That night, the old vixen led them toward the west, in the direction the rain usually came from.

Here lay the most broken-up ground of this old forest. The rocky substrata had pushed up through the light cover of grassy earth. Silly rabbits leaped about on the mossy rocks that the moon now covered with a blue light.

The four hunters ran along, the cubs' noses trembling with the nearness and richness of so many scents. They stopped and lay flat where the clear spaces began, their eyes glistening and their mouths wet with appetite. But their mother cuffed them along. "Further, further on," she insisted.

They climbed down rocky ravines, breathing as they went the smell of cold water sweated from the roofs of caves lined with bats. Old oaks with contorted roots and wrinkled trunks stood widely separated, softened by the white light.

The little ones were carried along by their mother's haste. They had a hard time following, but they didn't want to lose her in the midst of these tormented shapes so different from the softness of their own familiar valley.

They crossed over the brook on gleaming stones, lap-

ping at the chill waters as they passed. Then came the upward climb, even harder than the downward rush. They went in a series of leaps up the unlit side of the hill. With these mounting shadows began the far country they had only glimpsed during their earlier hunts.

They had come to the heart of the forest. The rocks and oaks gave off multiple odors so rich they felt dizzy. It would have taken a dozen noses to recognize a single trail in this undergrowth.

Under these low branches lay patches of warm air that smelled of spicy plants. Squirrels had passed by there; so had weasels. Rabbits had left tracks and droppings, still warm.

The smell of man was still on the paths. The little ones pulled their heads between their shoulders. But their mother knew it was only the odor of harmless strollers, by her standards blind, deaf, and stupid in the ways of the forest. These men were useful only for making clumsy noises and frightening off the game.

This flat high place sloped gently. The first beech trees appeared. Their gray trunks lifted leafy branches high toward the sky. The stars hung beyond the leaves in bright clusters.

Suddenly the vixen stopped and lay flat. The little ones followed suit, eyes rolling, hearts pounding.

For a few seconds they stared into the dark, trying to see what danger menaced them. They noticed a stirring, as of shadows, slipping between the trees. It was a very subtle motion, hardly visible, scarcely a hint of moving gray on gray.

It was this motion that had halted their mother. She raised her head almost at once. This told the cubs that they were in no danger.

But their watchful mother still did not stir. Then they could hear light footsteps, and the sound of peaceful creatures passing close by. The cubs recognized the odors that now came to them. They glanced at the vixen. She had flattened down again, and they knew that these were creatures that foxes might sometimes take as their prey. Stronger and stronger, the odors stirred their hunting blood and alerted their wiry young muscles.

A form showed between two trunks. It stood wary and watching, intent on piercing the mystery of trees and luminous night. It was a deer.

The cubs looked up, impressed, from where they lay belly to the ground. The deer, ten times their size, loomed so near that they could see the shimmer of its hide, the nervous twitches of its short tail, the mistrustful wrinkling of its nostrils searching out the smells of the night.

After the male came the does. They in their turn entered into the round of moonlight, grazing here and there among the bilberry bushes as they came.

The whole herd filed past some two yards from the fox family. Fawns born that year stayed close to their mothers. Probably some alarm earlier that evening had alerted them to prudence. The vixen decided she didn't want to chase them. She had better plans for the night.

Deliberately, she stood into the wind. At the scent of four foxes the deer whipped close together and sped off in a pebbly clatter of wild flight.

The vixen gave her silent grin. The little ones leaped, laughing merrily too, eager for the feasts this night promised to provide for them.

They took up their trek again, as hard and fast as before. The small foxes had no idea where they were headed. They were tired of running, and they were hungry. The smell of meat had whetted their appetites.

They crossed over tracks of game so fresh that it made them yawn with hunger. Dreams of delicious feasting exploded in their heads. What was their mother thinking of! They hoped this race wouldn't go on all night long.

The moon was dipping down the other side of the sky. The shadows lengthened. The air grew cooler. Was dawn with its frosting of dew already near?

The countryside grew more uneven, more leafy. Here moonlight penetrated only the tall tops of the massed trees. Across the open spaces, long scarves of fog floated in the middle air.

Then the foxes smelled water. It seemed to be there before them, close by. Perhaps it lay hidden by the white fog they saw adrift over a wide wooded hollow under a great clear space of starred sky.

Foxes don't like still waters, whose squashy banks dirty their fur and crust it with mud that dries and drags painfully at their skin.

A dead odor of mucky land came to them, mixed with other unknown, disturbing smells. The little ones felt ill at ease and watched their mother. She, too, seemed uncomfortable. Standing at the mouth of the wood, she sniffed the air carefully. Ears pricked up, she listened long, as if she wanted to pluck from the night some special, expected sound that would re-assure her.

Following her example, the little ones thrust their muzzles forward and pricked their ears. They heard only thin, half-formed sounds, the scraping of reeds, the light slapping of little waves on mud, the creaking of a chain that anchored a rowboat.

Stare as they might, they saw nothing but the black of the trees and the white of the fog. But the lay of the surrounding countryside slowly took shape in their heads.

So far, they had realized that a house belonging to men lay near this water. They could distinguish the smell of stones giving back their day's warmth to the night, a whiff of smoke, flower smells from gardens. And now what? Had the long race through the night been for no reason but to visit this place? Why this house, when there were others at the opposite end of the forest, much nearer home? Their mother had taken them around the edges of men's farms and villages more than once. They knew the smell of men and of the stupid animals they kept about them. This was nothing new, so far.

Suddenly a sound rose out of the distance, fragile and pure, a sound they had never heard before. It seemed to ribbon out across the silence like a subtle scent, delicate and keen, that wove across the night. It rose and fell, like the flight of an insect whose buzzing goes and comes, circles off and returns. It drew their nerves taut and tensed them to the point of howling.

The mother rose. She seemed satisfied. So that was what she had been waiting for! She had expected this winged sound to surround them—a sound that came out of the depths of the night, then fled, melted into silence, only to soar up once more.

The little ones were dazzled by admiration for their mother's unfathomable wisdom. They did not know that during her long life the old fox had come this way thousands of times. And she had learned that her night was sure to be undisturbed while the Old Man played his violin.

With the cubs following in her tracks, the mother stepped calmly down the gentle slope that led to the pond. Out from the cover of trees, they found the air cold and water-soaked. The little ones shivered and peered around. Under the immense open sky they felt open to attack. They would have welcomed the friendly shelter of low-growing leaves. The freshness of the fog filled their nostrils. They could distinguish no odor other than the stinging scent of dew. They felt half blind, as if they were lost in shadows.

Yet the night was not black. They circled the pond where white vapors floated. Through the spaces between the reeds, reflections of sky on black water winked at them. They came to a wide, smooth lawn, where clumps of trees stood like big bouquets. Beyond them, a house appeared.

It was much bigger than the village houses of the plain. It had a roof with several points, a tower, and many, many windows. One was lighted. It was up in the tower. From this rosy gold glow that starred the night came forth the enchanted sounds that now and then made their throats tighten to a whimper.

Their mother had begun to trot off toward the trees that curved back beyond the house. The little ones took off after her at a gallop. They had just reached cover when a howl, very close, froze them with fright.

The vixen flattened herself against the trunk of a plantain tree. The music stopped. A dark silhouette appeared at the window. A voice cried, "Quiet, Taillefer, quiet." There was silence at once, scarcely broken by Taillefer whining deep in his throat. Then the music began again.

The little ones saw their mother grin. She got up and led them purposefully around the lawn about the house.

The smells of man and dog were everywhere here. Shivering, the little foxes were filled with an ancient terror. An unbearable desire to flee gripped them. But their mother kept them close to her, and made them follow the tracks, nose to the ground, filling their lungs with the mingled, hated smells. "The Old Man and Taillefer! The Old Man and Taillefer! Wherever, whenever you meet this smell, watch out. Your life is in danger. No place is safe, not bushes, or trees, or even your own foxhole. Take to your heels and flee them— the Old Man and Taillefer!"

Terrified, the cubs had a sense of being surrounded by frightful dangers. These scents were everywhere, one crossing another, multiplied, horrible. And that music from above, that wail no throat could contain, kept on and on. Something awful would happen. The sky might fall down!

But nothing happened at all.

"And now, I shall show you the enemy—Taillefer."

They went around the far side of the house, to a wide, well-fenced dog run.

Taillefer was there, suffering too.

The vixen didn't venture too close. But the little ones could see a small brown creature standing on his hind legs, against the fence. They made out the narrow oval of his skull, his long ears, his splayed feet.

As they slipped across the night, they could see, too, how the basset's blazing eyes followed them, hot with hate. They could guess at his hard breathing, his twitching nose, and the horrible fury that their presence evoked in him. Taillefer managed not to howl. But it took agonized efforts. He stood obedient and helpless, gnashing his teeth.

Taillefer!

For a long minute their mother let the little ones wallow in panic. Then she led them along the bank above the brook, pleased to notice that already their hearts were strong and their wind long. They walked a narrow ridge, squeezed between two high wooded slopes. Here in the undergrowth, the dense night was full of fresh and varied odors.

All the forest animals came to drink at Long Brook, and each left tracks of his passage.

But the cubs had only one wish, to put as much space as possible between themselves and the hate that had come across the night to them in the basset's whimperings. It was ancient and blood-borne hate, and they felt it still pursued them, beating in the very pulse of their blood.

Above, up there between the two dark crests of the ravine, the inverted river of the heavens ran more clearly. Dawn was approaching. If they didn't hunt soon, they'd be too late.

The vixen changed direction. Leaving the dark undergrowth behind, she led them in a climb toward the light. Soon the wanderers were at the top of the hill, where a sparse little wood of oak trees stood. Beyond the trees, suddenly, clear sky loomed overhead. They had reached the edge of the woods.

Before them spread the rounded back of a hill that turned into a gentle slope as it joined the spreading plain.

The moon lay very low, almost seeming to touch ground in some far land, dull, a dead star. At the other horizon a rosy stain heralded the coming of dawn.

The fox led her little ones across the plateau until they stood above the place where the hill sloped. Beneath them, halfway down the slope, stood a low building. It was unexpected and so close that the little ones stopped, frightened. They turned to their mother. She had lost the look of a strict and demanding teacher. Now she wore the unquiet, watchful expression of the hunt.

At the bottom of the hill, along the brook, was another man-house, surrounded by trees. The vixen paid no attention to it. She was lost in concentration on the hillside hut.

A prudent circular march brought them even with it. When they came into the wind, the little ones could smell fowl, lots of fowl. Appetite gripped them at once, tightening their bellies, filling their mouths with saliva. Breathing hard, they took cover along their mother's side.

The vixen looked long at the chicken house. Then she growled a little in her throat.

Finally, she made up her mind. She led the way down. Sniffing hungrily, the four brigands came up to the fence.

And that night, the door had not been locked.

III

Mascot sat on a chair between the twins. First one, then the other, gave him a crust of bread dipped in milk, made hot with sweet coffee. It wasn't simply a game. This was a regular breakfast ceremony that took place every morning.

Piet was stringing a new line, finer than the one he'd used before. In the next room, for no special reason, Tatie was singing "Roses of Picardy" as she did the housework. It was a morning like any other, peaceful, a little cool, a luminous morning. It filled the house with a gold and green clearness.

The sun had risen but was still below their hill. Splotches of light covered the forest slopes that faced east. A sharp cry cut across the air. No one paid it any heed. Tatie hummed away. Piet attached a fastener to a Number 8 hook with utmost care. Mascot swallowed his nineteenth bit of bread.

Suddenly Lina stood at the doorway, thin, tall, her hair wind-blown. She came in, fell into a chair, and groaned.

"Who's got troubles?" asked Tatie from the next room.

"Nobody," said Gerard.

"Yes, I heard a groan," said Tatie.

"It's Lina, the silly goof," called Piet.

"What's the trouble?" Tatie demanded, bustling in, a yellow scarf around her head. "Lina, for goodness' sake, what's wrong?"

Lina lay back, her head bent, her arms trailing, the very picture of despair.

"Idiot," cried Piet. But there was enough worry in his voice to make the twins and Mascot leap from their chairs.

"Oh, the chickens, it's the chickens . . . up there . . . dead . . . all of them," she sobbed.

"You're joking," said Gerard.

"Every one, all dead," Lina repeated. "They're strewn all over the place." She sat up sharply, as if trying to throw off a bad dream. "Come on, see for yourselves."

They saw a scene of slaughter, with bundles of feathers, blood, corpses, everywhere. Tatie, her lips tight, her face stone quiet, added up the extent of the disaster. Ten laying hens were gone, and half the turkeys, and heaven knows how many chicks. The horrified twins found some even outside the fence in the grass.

"Some animal did this," said Piet. "It must have been a weasel or a fox." He went beyond the fence and looked for tracks. There were plenty. A trail of

35

feathers lay scattered right up to the woods. A strangled white chicken lay under a bush. Still farther on were more feathers and blood-stained leaves. A hundred yards from the edge of the woods, he found a half-eaten carcass.

When he came back, the other children were standing together behind the henhouse. They ran to him.

"Where's Tatie?" he asked.

"She went back down."

"What did she say?"

"Nothing. She just turned and left, that's all."

"She didn't say it was our fault?"

"No, she didn't say anything."

"Well, it *is* our fault," said Piet, looking down and stubbing one sandaled foot into the dirt. "We must have left the gate open."

"Who did? Who was the last one out? I know I wasn't. I called you from up there," said Lina. They all remembered her waving her arms like a windmill above them.

Piet shrugged.

"Genevieve," said Lina in her sternest big-sister voice. Gerard began to sob.

"Don't be dense, Lina. What difference does it make which one left the gate open? It was left open; that's all that matters." Piet scowled fiercely at his sister.

"All right, then," said Lina. "But anyway, if Tatie asks, I can say it wasn't I. Nobody can contradict that."

"All right then, go ahead. Run tell Tatie, quick. Clear

yourself. It wasn't you. Go ahead, run. Who needs you around here, anyway?"

Lina took her injured feelings off quickly round the bend in the hill.

Piet, followed by the twins, inspected the premises again. He looked over the state of the fence and the roof, and came back to the gate.

Abruptly he turned to the twins and announced severely, "Now I don't want you to go telling Tatie it was you did it, or I'll come after you with my bow and arrow. Understand? One of us did it, and we don't know who, and that's all!"

"An animal did it," said Gerard.

"Yes, an animal," said Genevieve. "There are animals that eat chickens; it says so in the science book."

"Come this way. Let's have a look at the tracks," Piet said. As he went, he glared vengefully at the forest that hid the criminal behind its leafy screen.

As soon as she was out of sight of the others, Lina stopped. She plopped down into the grass and thought for a long while.

Once again she'd acted like an idiot; once again Piet had been right. This disaster was too big and too hopeless for babyish quarreling. No matter who had been guilty or how sorry they all were, there was no saving the situation. The guilty one could only be crushed by the enormous awfulness of his error.

"Not my fault," she thought. The fault had taken

place in a little tiny minute of absent-mindedness. Some-one hadn't shut a door properly. But the consequences! Ten laying hens, half the turkeys, and heaven knows how many chickens! Poor Tatie!

Lina flung herself flat on the grass and cried for all she was worth.

Meanwhile, Piet and the twins were tracking the killers, on all fours. There were no more feathers to follow, and the trail was harder to find. Farther and farther apart, a bit of fluffy down caught on a bush seemed to be a hint. But how could they be sure the down had come from the stolen fowl? It might come from some forest bird. How to tell?

Piet stood and stared, frowning at the wealth of undergrowth, the still trees, the bushes about him. He knew a thousand clues must be there. Dim recollections of things he'd read came to his mind, tales of Indians, trappers, cowboys. He'd read, hungrily, hundreds of stories of tracking, and always the hero could read signs in the grass or the dirt as if they were books. But Piet didn't know where to start.

"Hey, here's a passage," cried Gerard, showing a sort of hole in the growth under a bush. "And here's an-other!"

Perhaps they were really passages. But maybe they were only the natural spread of the branches. To Piet, this was the last proof of what he knew already. He was absolutely stupid in the woods—as ignorant as a baby. He had everything to learn.

"How about Mascot? Suppose we get him," suggested Genevieve.

"Mascot's no hunting dog."

"Maybe not a real hound. But he can find our tracks when we hide."

It was true enough. Mascot could track down the children in their most secret hiding places.

Led by the twins' hopeful enthusiasm, Piet went back toward the mill.

Lina arrived at the house determined to do something good to redeem herself. She expected to find Tatie in tears. She'd planned to throw herself into Tatie's arms and console her with a good cry together. Tatie would smile again, and Piet wouldn't have any reason to despise Lina any more.

This pretty plot didn't work out exactly as Lina had planned. When she came round the corner of the house, she saw Tatie sitting at the garden table, her head bent, preoccupied.

"She's doing her bookkeeping," thought Lina, slowing her steps. But Tatie wasn't doing accounts. She was cleaning a pound of lentils and whistling the lively tune of "The Drum Major's Daughter."

Lina, undecided, didn't know how to announce her presence. But Mascot saw her and ran toward her from under the table.

Tatie turned her head. "Do you like lentils?" She questioned, smiling. "I forgot to ask you."

"Yes, we do, yes, indeed we do, all of us."

This was no time for the children to dislike anything, Lina felt. She was ready to say she loved to eat whatever Tatie proposed, even escarole, which she hated.

She joined Tatie at the table, took a handful of lentils, and spread them before her.

She soon knew why Tatie had chosen this job to do. Separating lentils is very calming to the nerves. Tatie's agile fingers danced over the table, picking off a tiny stone or a bit of straw.

Lina tried to imitate her. But her fingers were trembling and wouldn't obey her.

Tatie didn't seem to want to talk. She had begun her wild whistling again. Now she'd got on to "O St. Hubert, Patron of Great Hunting Men." After three minutes, Lina couldn't stand it any longer.

"Tatie," she said, "don't tell the others, but I think it was me."

"You what?"

"Me that forgot to lock the gate. It's all my fault the chickens are dead."

"Who asked you anything?" exclaimed Tatie. "The chickens are dead, and that's that. There's nothing more to do or say. They might have died of cholera without anyone's having ever left the gate open. When you think of it, all this poultry is as messy as can be. They live or die, with hardly any reason at all. There's no counting on them; they have no sense."

The funniest thing was that Lina could really feel

Tatie was angry with the creatures. She was cross because they'd stupidly let their throats be torn out.

Tatie said, "Take the garden shovel and go ask Piet to make a big hole a way off from the chicken coop. You can bury those miserable cadavers in it. There's a useful thing to do."

When that job was done, the children led Mascot to the scene of the crime. He was a Parisian dog who had known nature, so far, only on the lawns at Buttes Chaumont Park. The discovery of real, unlimited natural life kept him hopping between a state of utter delight and a state of abject terror.

Now, at Piet's orders of "Hunt, hunt," Mascot put his nose to the ground and tried.

He followed tracks with self-abandon, working most conscientiously, here, there, and everywhere. Under clumps of daisies, at the roots of wild carrots, in a mole hole, around some bird droppings, he went. "Hunt, hunt." He was amazed at all the lovely things he could find when he really hunted for them.

Eyes bright, ears pointed, his plumed tail in the wind, the white dog leaped from one smell to another. More than anything else he reveled in the attention he was getting from his masters.

He barked for joy as he followed trails. Now and then he was distracted and jumped for a butterfly or one of the grasshoppers that leaped up out of the grass like sparks.

But suddenly, he came to a dead halt. Some profound,

far-off part of his being stirred strangely. He had come on a scent, strong and still fresh, that he somehow recognized, though he'd never smelled it before.

The age-old hunting instinct that slept in his blood had sprung alive at the cold scent of a fox.

He barked two or three times, with so new a voice he surprised even himself. "Yap yap yap," he snapped, instead of his usual "Woof woof."

He gave Piet a questioning glance. Piet, delighted, had heard the new note.

"Hunt, Masky boy, hunt. There, that's the way. Go to it."

Piet pointed, waving the dog on. By chance, it happened to be in the right direction. Mascot, nose to the ground, galloped toward the forest.

An hour later, the children and their dog stood in the midst of a clearing, undecided what to do next.

A few times, one or the other of them had got separated and had had to cry "Halloooo" to find the others.

"It would be easy to get lost, this deep in the forest," said Piet. "We'd better be careful."

The children had already noticed how easy it would be. In fact, in a way, they were lost already. Piet was the only one who realized that the brook they had just crossed was the same one that ran under Tatie's house.

From the central clearing where they stood, five paths led off into the woods. They were scarcely more than sketchy tracks among the trees. But they brought to mind a feeling of limitless, unmarked distances, scary loneliness, and calls for help.

The twins stood close to Lina, who wasn't feeling any too safe herself. Piet and Mascot were peering into the nearby underbrush.

At first, the hunt had been easy and excited. But Mascot had soon found himself hopelessly confused by the dozens of tracks leading crisscross in all directions. Quite a few foxes had passed that way through the forest. Mascot, with only an unused instinct to guide him, couldn't tell one from the other. He'd dashed about in several directions, retraced his steps, stuck his nose into a badger hole, and, finally, lost all the fox scents. Now he was following any trail he happened on, rabbit, deer, or badger. He was furious at finding nothing.

Finally, he did find something. In the hollow of a bush, at the foot of a log, there was some living creature. Mascot barked so hard, dashing back and forth, that Piet was convinced. He called his brother and sisters to see the end of the hunt.

Beside himself with excitement, Mascot tumbled like a wild thing, yapped, started to leap, and fell back whimpering.

"There's something there," said Lina. "That's sure."

Piet armed himself with a stick and cautiously parted the thick leaves. At first, in the shadow, he could only see an inextricable tangle of branches and thorns. But finally he thought he saw an animal shape.

He pushed his stick at it. He felt a resistance that was at once soft and compact.

"A hare," he cried.

But just then a ray of sun slipped through the leaves.

The light struck a rounded chestnut-colored lump. It was only a hedgehog.

The afternoon wore away. The children were dismal and dull, and no one felt quite himself. They came and went, not knowing what to play or do. They watched Tatie, determined to be marvelously well behaved from now on. One word would have been enough to start a deluge of tears that might have lightened the atmosphere and made everyone easier.

But Tatie went on as if nothing had happened. She kept busy, laughing and singing as usual. It was dreadful.

Piet gave up first. He took his rod and went off to the brook after trout.

Lina went to her room, saying she'd write the letter she owed her English pen-pal, Coral Tenoaks.

The twins could find nothing better to settle down with than their summer study notebooks.

Only Mascot kept Tatie company. He still had a tiny spot of blood on his nose. When Tatie began to knit, he sat at her feet. But he soon slept, haunted by dreams of heroic hunting.

He slept on, making half-stifled sounds that echoed his dreamed exploits.

Toward four o'clock, Tatie went into the dining room and found the twins at the table, heads between their hands.

"Well? Isn't anyone going to have an afternoon snack today?" she asked.

The two redheads exchanged a sad look. Genevieve shook her head.

"Why ever not? Are you sick?"

"No, it's Gerard. He has something to tell you."

"What is it, Gerard?"

"Umhu," said Gerard, and lowered his head miserably.

"Oh, no," said Tatie.

"Oh, Tatie," cried two voices at once. "We're the ones."

"I stayed the last . . ."

". . . and then the wind pushed the door."

"We thought it was closed fast . . ."

". . . so we just walked away and left it like that."

They were hopping around like two agitated elves, their wide, anxious eyes on Tatie.

Tatie put her hand over her ears and burst out laughing.

"Really?" she asked.

"Yes, yes, that's just what happened."

Tatie looked at them for a moment, obviously embarrassed. "But just what is it you're talking about, my dears?"

"About what? About the chickens, of course."

"Ho," said Tatie, shrugging her strong shoulders. "What are a few chickens, more or less!"

"And the hens, Tatie?"

"They were old, you know, and not good for much anyhow. I'm glad to be rid of them, when you get right down to it."

The redheads weren't sure whether Tatie was serious

or not. Tatie knew they didn't quite believe her. But the important thing just now was to act as though what she had said was the whole truth. The important thing was to be together and laugh again.

Tatie covered their small faces with her large hands so they couldn't see her face, and, with tears in her eyes, she laughed and laughed.

The cry of a night bird woke Piet from sleep. It sounded like "Tioulou . . . crcrcr! Tioulou . . . crcrcr!" The forest was so near that his room seemed nested among trees. Through the open window, the night air carried every least sound right into the room.

An animal gave two quick series of barks. Piet leapt to the window—a fox? a badger? a boar? What was it? Once more, Piet accused himself of ignorance about this wild world around him. He had everything to learn about the insects, plants, and beasts of the forest.

He saw light across the trunk of the red maple to the left. The lights of the big living room must still be on. He lifted himself over the window sill and went round the house.

Tatie sat at the table, deep in her account books. Piet watched her a moment.

It was certain that the loss of the poultry had been a catastrophe for her. She had counted on the sale of the young chickens and turkeys to pay off a good part of her debts.

All day she had pretended to be calm, for the

children's sake. Piet longed to help her solve her problems.

He considered what he could do to help Tatie out of this tight corner. Of course, he could write to his parents and ask them to pay back what their carelessness had cost. But he knew that wasn't a really good idea. Tatie would positively despise him if he worried his parents now.

No, he'd have to find another way. And first of all, he'd have to settle with the murderer. The thieving creature would surely come back to the scene of his crime. And Piet would be prepared to give him a suitable reception.

Traps, poison, sticks, stones—anything would do that might bring about the annihilation of the killer.

IV

For almost a week, the fox family feasted on the spoils they had taken from the chicken yard. Their loot was well hidden in hollow logs and under bushes, camouflaged by layers of dead leaves. The young foxes needed only a sniff of it to bring back their glorious night of slaughter. It was, for them, an endlessly exciting memory.

But, no matter how excited they were, their mother was very cautious. Whenever they neared their hidden treasure, she would hold them back with a snarled command. If they approached it too close, too fast, she roughly cuffed them aside. Every time, before touching their prey, she insisted on going up to it alone, sniffing and peering all around.

"What's the matter with her?" thought Bigson. "Everybody knows how game should be approached. She's showed us hundreds of times. Besides, this game is dead. We're not stupid, after all. She's so old, she's silly."

One night, Bigson came upon one of his own hiding places. It was in the forked hollow of an elm log. His mother warned him to slow down. But Bigson snarled and kept right on.

That started a real fight. The smaller foxes watched, horrified. The old vixen was furious. She punished her son so thoroughly that he could only whimper his anger. He decided to leave his family, once and for all. Off he ran, beaten and bad-tempered.

Up a sharp slope he sped, as fast as he could go. He wanted to leave his mother far behind.

He didn't stop until he came to a brook. There, he lapped at the cool water and grew calmer.

Along the banks of the brook, the night seemed especially dark. Treetops met and interlaced to form a huge black arch overhead. Beneath it, the water tinkled, gleaming faintly here and there. The air was dank and heavy.

Bigson shivered. He didn't like these damp, dark places. His fur was soaked with dew and tangled with sticky burrs and leaves.

He couldn't leap the brook. It ran too wide. He began to look around for a way to cross toward the clear woods. Somewhere there was a row of wide, easy stepping-pingstones. His mother always found it without any trouble. He wished he'd paid more attention to her when he had the chance.

But he wasn't worried. He knew he'd manage single-handed, never fear. He trotted up the bank, sharp-eyed, his muzzle to the wind. He hadn't gone far when he saw the brook widen out into a sort of pond. Beyond the pond lay a house.

Bigson stopped, his heart pounding. It wasn't the Big House, where the Old Gentleman and Taillefer lived. This one was smaller and closer to the water. In fact, he soon saw that it was right on the water.

Prudently, he made a tour of the silent and shadowy grounds, skirting the border of trees. He heard nothing new, save the sound of water dripping from an arm of the windmill.

A complicated mixture of scents told him men were present here. But men sleep at night and are no longer dangerous.

Suddenly a wild volley of barks burst from the house.

The startled fox scrambled off at a gallop. In a flash he reached and crossed a little bridge. It led into a road along the flat farmlands, where all sorts of delicious poultry lived.

Bigson knew this territory. Already roosters were beginning to announce the new day. He smiled at the sound, but he hesitated to venture into the broad open spaces. He kept to the side of the road, following a ditch under the trees.

Abruptly, he stopped. Right before him, on the suddenly lit-up road, lay his own shadow. He wheeled around to see two yellow suns, close to the ground and coming toward him in a strange roar of noise.

Amazed and unable to see, the fox ducked and shut his eyes. When he opened them again, the Thing was almost abreast of him. It sped past in a growl of thunder and enveloped him in a gust of warm air.

Bigson shivered and dove off into the underbrush. He

stopped on higher ground, at the edge of a neat, light pinewood. Dawn flooded the air with its tranquil watery light.

A herd of does came up from their lower pastures and headed for the heart of the forest. A stag followed, a great lone fellow whose branching antlers tangled with the low branches of the trees. Twice the stag stopped to scratch his back slowly against a tree. He had just been drinking at Long Brook. His nostrils were wet, and bright threads of water sparkled on his chin.

The pinewood seemed to be a sort of public crossroads, where all the animals passed on the way home to their lairs.

As Bigson watched, a family of badgers filed by. There were Mr. Badger, Mrs. Badger, and their children, sleek and shiny with good health.

On their heels came an old graying fox. When he scented Bigson, he gave him a haughty nod and went on.

Overhead, squirrels leaped from branch to branch with sharp little cries.

The forest was waking up. A weasel ran by at top speed.

All these creatures had finished their night's hunting and were headed home with full bellies.

All at once, Bigson realized that he was hungry. He'd eaten nothing since the previous day.

Anger at the remembered beating he'd taken from his mother brought him to his feet. He had to admit he was just as angry with himself. Since he'd claimed his free-

dom, he'd done nothing but rush aimlessly around, to no
good. It was time for him to do some serious thinking.

Daylight filled the forest. Hunting hours were over.

Driven by hunger, Bigson hurried off, searching right
and left. But his approach drove off every other creature. Birds flew up with shrill cries. Squirrels chattered.
Every creature was warned that a killer was coming,
and fled to safety.

The fox felt the stare of hundreds of nervous eyes.
His passing brought the whole forest to attention. But
soon the other animals realized that Bigson was only a
young, inexperienced hunter, and they ran off noisily
ahead of him.

Bigson ate a beetle and a lizard, and at last he caught
an absent-minded mole who was still tunneling, although

the sun was up. The fox saw bits of loose dirt rolling
from the humped ground. He leaped furiously on the
tunnel and seized the mole before it could disappear into
its underground maze.

It was a poor, mean victory and a poor, skimpy meal.
But even that little success changed Bigson's mood. He
felt he had proved his independence, and rejoiced.

He thought about his mother, though. He needed to.
He had to remember what it was she did when the sun
stood high. Usually, she'd find a warm, sheltered spot
and sleep.

Good enough. He, too, would sleep.

On a rocky valley slope, where the powerful roots
of ancient oak trees rose like great serpents from the
earth, Bigson found his place. He chose a flat, sun-

warmed rock, sheltered from the wind. He rolled up into a crown and fell asleep, his head pillowed on the bushy spread of his tail.

That day, Piet had left the house at midmorning. He'd already helped the other children with their studies. Neither Lina nor the twins had asked to come with him. Mascot had barked for joy to see him get ready to go out, so Piet had decided to take the dog along.

The excuse for the outing was to gather mushrooms. But Piet didn't expect to find any. The farmer who brought their milk had said that the summer had been much too dry; there'd be no mushrooms until after September's heavy rains.

The real reason was that Piet wanted to explore the woods. He hoped to make himself familiar with some of its landmarks. The family outings later on would be more fun if he knew his way about. At the same time, this would be a good chance to find out things about the forest animals, and how they live.

Toward noon, the boy and his dog found themselves deep in the forest, not far from the rocky valley where Bigson slept on his rock.

They had come a long way without stopping and had wonderful appetites for lunch. Piet wished he'd brought along a few extra sandwiches. After sharing the last crust of what he had with Mascot, he was still hungry. Mascot looked up sidewise at him, as if inviting him to pull another sandwich from his pocket. But the pocket was empty. Piet pulled out the lining and shook it.

Mascot snapped up the crumbs as they fell. Then, making the best of it, he curled up and slept.

It was warm. Midday sun shone straight down on the still leaves. It was quiet, save for a ceaseless rustling made up of thousands of tiny, sparklike forest sounds. The fragrance of hot resin mingled with the stronger smells of bark and mosses. Now and then, a drift of fresh air swirled among the trees, bearing an odor of ferns.

Piet stretched out on the carpet of brush that covered the ground. It was a rough bed, but he was sleepy. He slept at once, before the white cloud he'd glimpsed had had time to cross the blue space between the oak leaves that sheltered him.

For some seconds, the landscape wavered before his eyes, as the banks of a pond seem to waver where they are reflected.

Piet shut his eyes again, opened them, shut them, and decided to wait until his dreams cleared away. He had a sketchy, dreamlike image of a man sitting in a cloud of smoke.

When finally Piet opened his eyes once more, he saw the man before him, sitting under a tree, pipe in mouth, turning a yellow cane in the dirt between his feet.

Piet half sat up, his mind hazy, his eyes blurred. He didn't know quite what to think.

"Easy, son," said the man in a quiet voice. "There's no hurry."

He picked up a twig, poked down his tobacco, and puffed away.

Piet continued to look up at him, amazed. The man took the pipe from his mouth.

"I hope you'll forgive me," he said. "I should have realized how surprised you'd be to see me here."

Mascot sprang up just then and began to chase his tail, barking.

"My apologies are extended to your dog, too, young man. What is his name?"

"Mascot, sir."

"Mascot? A good name." From beneath a weathered hat, the stranger's bronzed face showed a network of lively wrinkles that gathered into fine smile-lines around his eyes. They were bright blue eyes, with a merry young look.

He rose to his feet. He wore hunting clothes, with wooden buttons, and tan leggings, and carried the yellow cane.

Piet rose too, a little embarrassed.

"I allowed myself to intrude," said the old man, "because of this." With the tip of his cane he lifted a kind of crimson ribbon from the ground and held it toward Piet.

The boy took one look and stepped back.

"Don't worry; it's quite dead. It's a crimson viper. Luckily, I was passing by just as it was about to reach your neck. It would very probably have crawled right over you without doing any harm, especially if you hadn't stirred. But I was afraid you might make some unfortunate move. If you had . . ."

"Oh, and I'm sure I should have!" cried Piet, with a shudder. He bent over the viper's body. "Their bite is fatal, isn't it?" he asked.

"Yes, especially if they bite in the region of the neck."

"Sir," Piet stammered, "I . . . I don't know how to say . . . to thank you . . ."

"Nonsense, nonsense. . . . Don't trouble yourself. It was nothing, and you owe me nothing. I saw before me two self-sufficient existences. I chose to act in favor of preserving yours as being the more precious of the two. Nothing to it."

Piet, somewhat surprised by the old gentleman's light tone, couldn't think how to answer. He suspected the man was making fun of him.

Mascot, having made a careful, complete survey of the stranger, came up and nosed his head under the browned, wrinkled hand.

The man took him by the muzzle and shook it in a friendly way.

"Good dog, Mascot. I knew another Mascot once. He was a baboon, and he could fill my pipe for me as well as a Chinese servant. I was sorry when I lost him."

"Did he die, sir?"

"I suppose so. The last time I saw him was in 1910."

"Do baboons live to be very old?"

"Let's see, now; yes, 1910 it was; and Mascot was between the jaws of a shark. That was the last glimpse I had of him."

57

"Poor Mascot!" said Piet.

The live Mascot, happy as a lark, was nuzzling the man's hands and growling low in his throat with pleasure.

"Easy there," said the man, smiling. "You're going to get on Taillefer's nerves."

Piet followed the man's glance. Some twenty feet away a brown dog crouched at the foot of a tree. He was watching everything that went on. His long snout and big droopy ears made him look serious as any judge. The attention he was giving Mascot and the pats his master was distributing made him look even more serious than that.

Taillefer had been sitting for fully fifteen minutes as still and discreet as a dog of stone.

Mascot hadn't even suspected his presence. When, on a signal from his master, Taillefer ran up on his short legs, Mascot was so taken aback that he bounced ten feet to the rear, bristly as a hedgehog, barking fit to strangle.

The man burst out laughing.

"The city mouse and the country mouse!" He chortled. "Now let's see you two get acquainted. Here, Mascot," he called, holding out his hand to Piet's pet.

Taillefer, who had been standing with two paws on his master's leggings, dropped down and turned away in a sulk.

Mascot came frisking up. The man took him by the collar.

"Taillefer," he murmured.

Taillefer turned at once and lifted his big tawny eyes to his master.

"Come, old friend; don't be jealous. Jealousy's a contemptible thing."

Full of dignity, the basset approached on his bowed legs, carefully ignoring Mascot.

"Taillefer, this is Mascot," explained the man. "Try to remember him, do. And don't try to strangle him in some dark corner of the forest. Understand?"

Taillefer slapped his tail on the ground several times in answer.

"Understand?" repeated the man.

"Ooyeah," yawned Taillefer, in a big yawn that ended in a smile.

"Good!"

"Do you think he really understood?" asked Piet.

"Indeed he did," the gentlemen answered. "Taillefer may not always be easy to get along with, but he's very intelligent. Aren't you, Taillefer?"

"Ooooyeah," yawned Taillefer again.

Piet laughed for all he was worth.

V

It would be too much to say that the two dogs became the best of friends at once. But Mascot was so glad to have found a companion that Taillefer put up with his friendliness without showing too much disgust for his antics.

After a few quiet questions from the man in hunting costume, Piet began to talk. He explained who he was, who Tatie was, and why some of his family had come to stay for a while at Long Brook Mill.

"You're fairly far from the mill now. Would you like me to set you off in the right direction?" asked the courtly old man.

Piet was glad to agree, and they started off together, the dogs following.

No walk Piet had ever taken was more pleasant.

As they went, the man followed the animal trails they crossed with his eyes, as if he knew all the habits of the woodland creatures and was accustomed to taking them by surprise in their natural setting. Now and then, he'd stop and hold out his cane, as if silently retelling the story the forest was telling him.

Piet watched and looked and peered, but saw only a space between some bushes or the intertwined masses of the treetops in an infinite series of shades of green.

Piet didn't dare disturb the walk with questions. His companion seemed hardly to know he was there. Occasionally Piet heard him breathing more heavily and murmuring a few words, as if to himself.

Once, the man stopped and pointed out a tree with a smooth, straight trunk that rose like a shaft to its tangle of branches against the sky. The branches, at one point, made an arabesque design like a golden filagree. Another time, he pointed off to the side toward an eruption of dark red earth across the flank of a ravine; it was like a blood-hued scar where violet tree shadows danced.

But was the man really showing these things to him? Piet couldn't be sure. His companion's every gesture was rich in an ease and a wisdom beyond Piet's grasp. Besides, the man was the absolute opposite of an insistent teacher. "Take what you will," he seemed to be saying.

It was the onset of evening. The forest hummed. Flights of clear-winged insects danced in light. Long sunrays slanted across the high leafage and played across smooth trunks as if they were columns of ancient stone.

"Sir," Piet said abruptly, "are there foxes in this forest?"

The man smiled. "Foxes? Ah, indeed, foxes and deer, stags, badger, wild pigs, squirrels, marten, and otters— to say nothing of rabbits and birds, nor, of course, of elves and gnomes, nor of the Sleeping Beauty, nor of talkative old men like me! But seriously, I imagine I know what would please you. You'd like to see some of this wild life for yourself, wouldn't you? With a little luck, I might be able to show you one or two creatures. At any rate, I can show you the signs they leave for us to recognize them by.

"Here, for instance, are signs of our rabbit friends. They make no secret of their whereabouts and their excellent digestion. Look here."

With his stick he showed Piet the many little grayish marbles of ordure scattered on the ground.

"They had a big gathering last night. I shouldn't be surprised if someone, perhaps a fox, joined the party."

He cast his quick glance about. "Their holes are over there in the briar patch. Let's go look."

A moment later they could see traces of slaughter— a few drops of blood, a few tufts of soft fur.

"The fox began his wait here, behind this thick briar bush next to the hole. See, the grass is still bent over. He waited until the hole's owner showed up, murdered him, and took him off over his shoulder."

Piet didn't say a word. He was imagining the pinewood by moonlight and the gay, stately dance of little white-tailed rabbits on the smooth ground. It made him sad to imagine their games over and one of them dead.

"The fox is a cruel creature, isn't he?"

"Well," said the man coolly, "he's a tough customer."

"But why does he hurt poor harmless rabbits?"

"Since the days of the Garden of Eden, you can't say anything is harmless. The rabbits would destroy the forest, if there were no foxes. It's all a question of balance."

The man held out his expressive hands, as if he were demonstrating a most delicate balance: the plants of the forest on one side of the scale, and on the other, the entire race of rabbits.

"It's all held in a marvelous equilibrium. Sometimes men try to break up that balance. But they pay dearly for it when they do. Balance is the key to everything. But man has never had sense enough to be content with things as they are."

They had come to a pinewood full of sun that stood above a narrow valley, where shadows were already advancing.

Over on the other side of the valley, big, widely spaced oaks spread their strong roots to grip the rocky soil where strands of briar crept.

The man stopped, half hidden by the low branches of a pine. He beckoned Piet close and took him by the shoulder.

"Look there, before you, on the slope," he whispered. "Do you see anything specially interesting?"

Piet's glance went from the sunny height to the handsome bronzed oaks, the gilded rocks, and the ruddy briar.

"I see trees, rocks, briar bushes . . ."

"Good. Now stretch out your arm, this way. Point your index finger; that's it. And close your left eye. Spot the trunk of the third oak next to that big tuft of yellow flowers at the foot of the pointed rock. Do you follow me?"

"Yes."

"Block off about half of the oak tree and look to the right of your finger, just at its edge."

"I see," said Piet. "There's a flat rock with a russet spot on it."

From his vest pocket the man took a pair of binoculars that he put in Piet's hand. At first he couldn't make them work; he saw only a whitish circle, rayed around the edges. Then forms appeared, and he saw, as if ten feet away, the split trunk, the knotty roots, the flat rock, and there, on the rock . . .

"Oh!" he said. "It's a fox. He's asleep; no, he's waking, he's yawning, he's scratching his neck, he's stretching!"

"He's a young one," said the man. "An old hand would never let himself be surprised this way. I'd bet he has no lair of his own yet. We'll give him a little lesson. Hold your dog, please. Taillefer!"

Taillefer came to attention, muzzle pointed, eyes wary. His master showed him with gestures the slope and the way across to it.

"Go to it, boy," he said.

Bigson opened his eyes and shut them at once. A shaft of light had entered to show him his familiar world of trees. But the sun hurt his eyes. A trace of childishness made him confusedly half fear the forest with its loneliness and ambushes. He lazed, enjoying the soft warmth on his eyelids.

The stone was warm; his fur, soaked with sun, was warm; the odors floating at ground level were warm too.

But sleep was leaving him. He yawned a long yawn, stretching his stiff paws, whose extended claws scraped along the stone.

He scratched at his neck, thick with heavy fur where sharp-biting parasites hid. He yawned again and whimpered a little.

Suddenly, barking filled the ravine. Down there, something white had surged up out of the black undergrowth and was heading up the slope in erratic leaps across the bushes.

Bigson's first impulse was to flee with all speed. But he soon realized that this bounding barker wasn't very dan-

gerous and anyway didn't seem to be headed for him.

What had happened was that Mascot had escaped from Piet's hands and taken off after Taillefer. Taillefer was going toward Bigson indirectly, in a wide curve, out of the wind that might warn the fox.

Flattened against a log, Bigson carefully watched the route of the white dog. Suddenly he noticed, slipping through the brush, the furtive shape of the basset.

In a flash he recognized the monster he had seen in the dog run at the Big House. Terrified, he bounded away, disappeared, reappeared farther off, vanished once more,

then sprang forth like a red flame, and finally plunged
up the other slope.

Behind him, the two dogs led him a devilish race.
Mascot had never in his life had such a great time.
While Taillefer followed the trail, Mascot dashed right
and left, beside himself with excitement. He barked at
echoes, got lost, found the track again. He even threw
himself, just for fun, onto the basset, who brushed him
off with a furious "*Yap!*"

It was useless for Taillefer to protest. Mascot found
the game so exciting, he had to demonstrate his joy.

Somehow he managed to grab one of Taillefer's paws. It was a perfect tackle. The two tangled dogs rolled down the slope in a duet of howls made up of Mascot's sharp cry of "Yi, yi, he's torn my ear off," and Taillefer's thunderous voice announcing, "Ooof, oof, for the love of heaven, someone get this idiot out of my hair."

The man began to laugh. "Poor old fellow, it's the first time you've gone hunting in the company of a clown."

"I'm sorry," said Piet. "Mascot's sure to spoil everything."

"Nonsense!" The man laughed. "It's only a game— and Taillefer really has so little sense of humor, it may do him good."

Now the hunt was on the far slope of the hill. The man listened a moment.

"There are dozens of foxholes over there, and I'd be surprised if— There! hear that? Taillefer's announcing that the quarry has gone to earth. Let's go see how their hunt looks."

It looked very simple.

Bewildered by the cries of his followers, Bigson had dashed into the first hole he came to. Unluckily for him, it was an old one, long abandoned and coming to pieces.

Twice his length under earth, he came up against a fall of earth. The earth was soft and dry, and Bigson managed to push through it. He found himself in a fairly large underground room that soon filled with his heavy panting. His heart pounded wildly. He imagined red faces grimacing in the black of his refuge. After a while his body grew calmer.

But he'd hardly started to catch his breath when Taillefer's triumphant cry echoed at the entrance to the hole. Almost at once he heard his enemy's breath at the other end of the corridor.

In fright, he hurried toward the first exit he could find. He saw daylight and headed for it until he saw a shadow across the threshold and heard another wild bark.

It was Mascot, who had just discovered the other entrance to the tunnel and was encouraging himself to head into it. What a shock for a Paris dog when he got a good faceful of the hot fox scent!

Horrified, he dragged himself back out, looking for aid. Seeing Piet and the man arrive, he barked hard to say that the quarry was at hand, that he'd almost got his nose nipped, and that the wicked creature stank like all the devils of the underworld.

"Well, well," said the man, "your Mascot is beginning to understand that these games are sometimes real."

"Is the fox really in there?" Piet asked.

The man calculated the distance between the two dogs and marked the spot with his heel.

"He's probably right here," he said. "He's shaking with fear, slammed against the floor of the room. I don't believe there are any exits. It's a very old hole. This poor youngster must be very inexperienced to have chosen it as a refuge. There's no reason for going on with this. Taillefer would just make a mouthful of him. I'll have to call a halt. The contest is too unequal."

He knelt before the entrance and whistled a command. Nothing happened. After a moment he said, "What the dickens!"

He was suddenly anxious. He whistled again and called, "Taillefer, Taillefer, Taillefer, come boy."

It was two or three minutes before the dog finally appeared. Until he did, the man had stayed anxiously bent over the opening.

Taillefer shook himself hard. He was covered with dirt and sand up to his eyes. He sneezed and shook and blew out his nose energetically. Then he was ready to receive his master's affectionate pats.

"A dirty mess, eh, boy. I wonder what happened. Half the tunnel fell in, I imagine. You might have stayed buried there for good, old friend."

His brown hand caressed the shapely dirt-splotched head, came down over the eyes, and stopped briefly over the muzzle. The man's voice murmured indistinct words that the dog clearly understood.

Piet could sense how much the dog and his master meant to each other.

Mascot was still on guard in front of the other exit. From time to time he threw himself on the opening, scratched the earth furiously, making dirt fly for three feet behind him. Then, he'd stick his nose in, breathing in big snores, and, half suffocated, throw himself backward, spitting with disgust.

"If you're agreed, we'll let the fox go," said the man.

"We'll leave the silly youngster in peace. No doubt we'll meet him again. Truth to tell, he seems born under a lucky star. The earthslide that almost smothered Taillefer saved his life. One should never go against such chance accidents. What do you think?"

"I don't know," Piet said. He stopped to think for a moment. "Is bad luck a warning too?" he asked.

"I don't doubt it," answered the old man. "Have you had a piece of bad luck?"

"Yes," said Piet. "It's a sad story called 'The Tragedy of the Unlocked Door.' It should have been shut tight, but it was left open."

"But it was left open?"

"Yes."

"And that caused a catastrophe?"

"Yes."

"I see," said the man, taken by Piet's solemn air. "When you stupidly throw a stone up into the air, it may very well fall down and hit you on the nose."

"Of course," said Piet. "And is that bad luck?"

"No. That's stupidity, pure and simple, for it's true, isn't it, that no one is obligated to throw stones in the first place?"

Piet's adventures in the forest took a whole evening to tell. Yet what he told was not a complete account of what had actually happened.

He never mentioned the deadly red viper. And he spoke of the Old Gentleman and Taillefer only vaguely as "a hunter and his dog." But he did describe the forest in full detail. There was the great discovery of the fox on the sun-warmed rock; there was the exciting chance that Mascot might learn to hunt; there was the siege of the fox's lair.

Why was it that he didn't feel like talking about the Old Gentleman? He didn't really know.

But he did feel that this had been more than just a casual encounter. That Old Gentleman had really and truly saved his life.

He had come on the scene just when the viper had reached Piet's neck. Piet was sure that the touch of the cold creature would have made him start in his sleep. He was just as sure that then the viper would have bitten him. Such a perfectly timed arrival seemed more than an unimportant accident.

Besides there was something strange and wonderful in the Old Gentleman's stately manners, in his language, in the deep affection between him and his dog.

All these things made Piet decide to say little about that part of his day. It was like a private treasure he'd discovered and had decided to keep to himself, at least for a while.

To make up for it, he tried to make the others share fully in Mascot's exploits. Every time Mascot heard his name, he looked up pleased, hoping for a chance to leap onto someone's knees.

Piet, usually a miser with words, proved to be a first-class storyteller. More than anything else, this proved how deeply his walk had excited him.

The younger children felt his excitement, too. Their

lively imaginations made dozens of plans for an expedition to find the fox's stronghold.

It was late. Tatie sat a little to the side, knitting. A lamp whose shade glimmered with multicolored butterflies shone on her work.

Beside her, an armful of leafy branches rose up from a big brown earthenware jar. Tatie loved to decorate the place with leaves that brought the soft breath of the woods into the house.

The room was so big that its corners vanished into shadow. Around the table, the children sat in an island of light. Just beyond the open windows, the forest lay cool and fresh. Now and again an animal cry or the call of an owl broke the quiet.

"Hush," said Lina. All together, they listened to the vast rumors of the mysterious night.

VI

"We must do something," said Lina. "Tatie's really flat broke. It must be awful for her. This was a terrible blow to her business. And the worst part is that she's not sure she's doing anything right any more. She said to me yesterday, 'For a grown woman, I'm a full-sized fool. Anyone who would set up a poultry yard just a few leaps from the forest isn't fit for much. I'll probably make even stupider mistakes before I'm through. Maybe I should give up the mill, and my independence, right now.'"

Piet reflected. Yes, it was a big piece of capital that Tatie had lost. But if she were to sell her new equipment, she wouldn't get half what it had cost her. The whole situation would be worse.

"Tatie could do anything anywhere and make good at it," said Lina. "But she'd always be sorry if she had to give up this house."

Piet said indignantly, "Who's going to make her give it up?"

"Well, if she sells the poultry equipment and all, she can't afford to live here."

"She mustn't think of selling, just because one fox was lucky, once."

"That's the trouble. She said it could happen again and again."

"It won't happen again, if we all work together. People are smarter and stronger than foxes, after all. We ought to be able to defend ourselves against them."

"You haven't got a gun."

"No, but we might get some hunters to help us get rid of the foxes, if we find their holes and show the hunters where they live."

Lina and Piet thought all afternoon, puzzling over the problem from all sides. That night at supper, they announced what they had planned.

They intended to declare war on foxes. Over a long distance around the mill, they would explore the forest carefully and destroy all the foxholes. They'd make life so hard for the chicken thieves that they'd have to leave the neighborhood. Tatie's poultry would thrive and multiply in peace.

They were so enthusiastic and confident that Tatie had to smile. "That's it," she said. "We'll just put up signs all over the woods, reading, 'We humbly request all Lord and Lady Foxes to withdraw from our vicinity and go hunt elsewhere.'"

"It isn't a joke, I promise you," said Piet. "We've thought it all out. We'll post a guard at the poultry yard for now. No foxes will dare come around."

With love in her voice, Tatie laughed. "So you're

going to keep watch? Wonderful. You'll take turns, I suppose? Who wants to be first?"

"Me, me," came the twins' twin cries.

"Fine," said Tatie. "The twins will begin. Go get your jackets on, my dears."

"Jackets? What for?"

"To wear on guard duty, of course. The nights are cold now, and it might rain before dawn. Go get your jackets, my good soldiers."

The soldiers seemed to have lost their enthusiasm. Puzzled, they glanced from Tatie to Lina and Piet. Must they really go out to do battle with the night, the cold, and the wind? It hadn't occurred to them that the job would be so frightening.

Everyone burst out laughing at their expressions of dismay. The same look of appalled amazement was on both faces.

"Let's be serious," said Lina. "Piet's idea is still good. We can scare the foxes off during the day. And at night we can leave poisoned meat around. The old lady at the farm told me that's what she'd do."

"Poison? Never!" said Tatie. "I wouldn't have poison around for anything. I'd rather suffer from all the foxes in creation than use poison. It's too dangerous. You can't aim poison. Besides, it's cowardly. I'd sooner buy a gun."

"Hey!" Piet exclaimed. "That's a great idea."

Tatie swallowed hard. She realized she'd better squash that particular enthusiasm.

"No," she said. "The best idea so far is to ask all the

76

local hunters to help. Maybe that fellow you met in the forest could come."

"What fellow?" asked Piet.

"You said you'd seen an old hunter and his dog in the woods."

The word "fellow" was so unsuited to Taillefer's master that Piet hadn't realized whom Tatie meant.

"Oh, yes," he said. "Tomorrow I'll go into the forest and have a look for him. I imagine he goes there often."

Piet didn't meet his friend in the forest. But the twins made a wonderfully interesting discovery.

Early in the afternoon, Tatie had taken the station wagon into the city to see what she could do about her money problems.

Lina, whose turn it was to write home, was in the living room.

Left to themselves, the twins had gone poking around, exploring an old shed they intended to clean out and make into their personal playhouse.

It was hard work. They pulled out old wormy boards, a wheel-less wheelbarrow, three flails for beating wheat, a big sieve with a hole in it, a willow fishing basket, and, finally, a bundle of old iron they couldn't identify.

They brought the bundle to Lina. She opened it. It held three rusty iron objects with great toothed jaws.

"Traps!" Lina exclaimed. "Just what we need for the foxes! Don't say anything to Tatie. She mightn't like traps any better than poison. She mightn't think they're fair—as if the foxes were fair to us!"

They spent several days after that getting the traps in working order. They removed the rust, and Lina brought some bacon from the kitchen to grease the springs and bait the traps.

Then, one evening, they announced that they were going for a walk. They picked the traps up outside. Piet had already chosen some spots in the woods that he thought foxes might frequent.

Jaws spread wide and springs ready for action, the traps were soon attached by their chains to tree trunks. Then the children camouflaged them lightly with twigs and dead leaves.

That evening, the children were particularly quiet and thoughtful. Each saw in his mind's eye some sly beast sneaking up on Tatie's chickens and being neatly strangled by a trap before it could kill a single hen. It seemed to them a satisfying idea.

In the middle of the night, loud crying startled the household from sleep.

It was Genevieve. She clung to Lina's neck, wailing, "Gerard, Gerard!"

It took several minutes to wake her and chase the nightmare. She wouldn't be quieted until Piet led Gerard in to see her, to prove he was unhurt.

Tatie was surprised. "She's not a nervous child. I've never known her to wake that way before. Genevieve, did you eat anything queer last night? Green walnuts? Wild berries?"

"No, no," Genevieve said with a sob. "It's the trap." She had dreamed she saw Gerard caught fast between the terrible iron jaws.

"Trap? What trap?" asked Tatie, wide awake now. "Has someone set out a trap?"

"Yes, for the foxes," said Piet. "The twins found three traps in the old shed."

"What were they like? Were they big traps?"

"About so big," gestured Lina.

"With teeth," added Genevieve.

"Heavens above, the wolf traps! And where did you put them?"

"In the woods, on passageways."

"Oh, no! We'll have to go get them, fast. What if someone were to come walking that way? Maybe some wretched person has been caught already and is lying unconscious out there with a broken leg."

"But, Tatie, we put them along animal passageways, not people's paths."

"That's not much better. Some poor beast may be slowly choking or struggling with its legs smashed. Piet and I'll get lanterns at once and take those traps out of there. Lina, you stay here and mind the twins."

When Tatie said, "At once," she meant it. A few minutes later, two little lights could be seen zigzagging up the hill toward the woods.

It was four o'clock in the morning.

Poor Piet—he was never able to explain afterwards what made him so dense that night. Was it the darkness that magically changed things? Was he mixed up because he had been wakened out of a deep sleep? Whatever the reason, he was utterly unable to find the traps.

Where he thought they'd be, there were no traps. It didn't help to think about it. It was a waste of time to try to remember the way they'd come the day before. He just couldn't seem to strike the right spots.

"Did you try to hide them from sight?" Tatie asked.

"Yes, under some dead leaves," Piet answered.

"But there are dead leaves everywhere. The traps could be any place in the forest. We'd better go right back to the house. You'll have to paint some big signs—at least a dozen—saying, 'Wolf traps—very dangerous.' Then you can put them up near the places you think you went last night. Put them where people passing by just can't miss them."

Life at the mill was a series of alarms and excursions after that. In spite of the dozen signs in a wide circle around the dangerous area, Tatie stayed on the alert every minute.

"Wasn't that someone calling out? Where are the twins? Where's Mascot gone to?"

Piet couldn't forgive himself. He burned secretly with self-accusing anger. If Tatie hadn't expressly and absolutely forbidden him to go into the woods, he'd have gone out alone. He'd have proceeded methodically until he found the traps. But Tatie wouldn't hear of it. She did agree that someday soon it would be a good idea to put on boots and make a slow, careful search, prodding the ground ahead of their feet with sticks. But she was too busy to go right now. It would have to be done the next week.

But something unexpected happened that speeded things up.

One afternoon, the twins went out to water the poultry. They came tearing back down the hill, shouting, "A dog, there's a dog in one of the traps!"

The family ran to the back of the house. They could hear barking, off and on, now close, now farther off. They thought it came from the dangerous part of the forest.

"Listen," said Piet. "It sounds like Taillefer."

"Who's Taillefer?"

"He's the dog I saw the other day. The hunter must be with him."

"I hope he can read," exclaimed Tatie, "and I hope he sees one of the signs before anything happens. Anyway, we'd better go find out."

When they were halfway up the slope, barking broke out close by. Mascot gave a joyous cry and was off like an arrow. Five different voices shouting "Mascot!" echoed through the valley. The excited dog took the noise as encouragement, ran even harder, and vanished into the forest.

"Quick, quick!"

"Mascot! MAAAscot!"

They heard more barking, then a dog's howls, followed by another dog voice yapping hard.

"There," Lina gasped in a scared voice, "he's trapped. I think I'm going to faint."

"Not now you don't," said Tatie, out of breath. "Sit on the grass until you feel better and keep the twins here. Slap her if she faints, twins. That will bring her to."

VII

After the earth walls of the abandoned lair had fallen in, Bigson lay shivering and still in the central room underground. The landslide that had covered Taillefer had fallen to the fox's left. He listened to the basset's terrible struggle to get free. Bits of earth rolled to a stop at his very feet. He expected at any second to see the monster appear in the shadows before him.

After a few tense moments, Bigson could hear only the barks of the silly white boaster who was guarding the other exit. When these barks, too, had stopped, he could hear only the hammering of his own heart. Among the good earth smells of the lair, vague traces of the feared scent of the menacing devil-dog remained.

Bigson stayed quiet a while longer, in a trance among the underground shadows. Finally his hope and confidence returned, and he felt the body heat flow back into his veins.

A confused memory of his mother crossed his mind. It came to him that he was really on his own now. It even seemed to him that he'd passed his first test fairly well.

He had stood up to the monster his mother had taught him was the most dreadful of his race's foes. And what had happened? The enemy had retreated. He, Bigson, had remained, master of the battlefield.

He grinned and yawned noisily. Suddenly he was hungry.

He went with caution to the exit. It was night in the immense, silent forest. Leaving the stuffy hole, he felt the sharp air penetrate his fur. He breathed deep. His nostrils took in, all at once, the thousand mingled odors of the forest.

Drawn up proud, on his haunches in the flat space before the lair, Bigson, drunk with joy, hurled his first hunting cry at the stars.

The next few days, however, taught him all over again that he was only a most ignorant, inexperienced youngster.

Several times, he came up against old lone foxes who chased him away savagely from foraging on their private territories. Driven by hunger, he longed to cross the frontiers these old hands had set up for themselves. But they had clearly marked their boundaries by depositing their own distinctive smells here and there. These odors said plainly, "Private property. No trespassing. Hunting strictly forbidden."

Bigson had to respect their meaning. Yet he was very hungry. His young, eager energies needed an abundance of food for fuel.

Finally, one night, he crossed a boundary line. He took up his defiant watch on the side of a briar patch where rabbits often congregated.

The master of this area was an old warrior who had conquered his domain in high combat. He knew perfectly well that a young intruder had been skirting his borders and made an inspection tour of his property every night. His own children had recently left him. But their mother still lived in a stronghold near his private underground castle. He let her stay, though she was bad-tempered and quick to take offense, because she was strong and just as sly as he. They were a fine pair of bandits who combined forces on winter nights to chase hurt or sick deer and force them to run until they dropped. These were the worthy persons to whom Bigson's unlucky star had brought him.

Flat to the ground in the shadow, he waited impatiently for the rabbits to show themselves. He could hear them chattering down inside their holes. He was so intent on his watch that he didn't notice the approach of two silent shadows slipping toward him downwind.

Suddenly a throaty growl burst out behind him. Bigson veered around, his jowls drawn back. Another grating sound came from his left. Two shapes with sharp-pointed ears were looking at him with obvious distaste.

"Gggra, ggra," snarled the first shape.

"Gggra, ggra," snarled the second.

"Grrrr," answered Bigson.

The growls began again, and the snarls deepened, wakening him to anger. He'd fight if he had to. Nothing in the world could make him retreat.

The vixen advanced on him.

Bigson leaped. It looked as though he might be going to run. But that was only a trick. Instead of disappearing, or answering her attack, he surged onto his other enemy who, surprised, rolled off under the shock.

Before the vixen could run up to help her spouse, Bigson had gotten in a few burning bites and was ready for more.

In the black dark, there was such confusion that it was hard to tell which was the enemy, and where. Bigson was able to withdraw honorably from a difficult spot. He crossed the slope and lost himself in the night.

The lordly old foxes, warned by the fight, doubled their watch against intruders.

So, driven from territory to territory, Bigson finally found himself on the edge of the forest, along the Long Brook where no fox would choose to make his home.

Hunger had become his most constant companion. He wandered, mud-splattered, always on the hunt, always hungry.

At night he trotted along the brook that led to the Big House.

The banks of the reed-bordered pond were the refuge of a few ducks and water hens. But there was no way to get at them, protected by their realm of mud and still waters.

Bigson had scarcely begun to step along the bank

when the birds woke and the voice of Taillefer sounded from down near the Big House.

The frightened fox retraced his steps. His tongue hanging out, he ran back as he had come. He stopped at the little house on the water. Here it was Mascot who recognized his scent and barked his head off.

Bigson ran off, a furtive shadow, yawning with impatience and hunger.

Wretched days these were, when he nourished himself on wild berries. The bushes scratched his nose and clung to his fur. He tried snails, without satisfaction. A viper bit his cheek, and the swelling shut his right eye. He was a sight.

One night he left the forest and made a wide tour of the countryside. It wasn't worth the effort. The dogs were sleeping out on the fresh straw of the new haystacks. He was spotted at once, and the whole village pack took after him. He had to get out in a hurry.

Once, coming back from an unsuccessful foray, he passed over the hill not far from Tatie's poultry yard. It was at dawn. He recognized the spot. Saliva filled his mouth. He went to sniff round the fence. But this time the gate was shut. Disappointed, he regained the cover of the trees.

And there, oh joy, he smelled an unknown smell so fine and so appetizing that he stopped still for fear it might vanish. He pointed trembling nostrils and sniffed, one after the other, all the currents of air that came to him. The scent was there, close, slight, but real.

He stood in a tiny clearing shadowed by a big aspen

with silvery leaves. His heart still, his attention riveted to the wonderful scent, Bigson took one step, another.

CRASH!!

Bigson leaped to the side. A violent jerk threw him on his back. Pain beyond measure sped through him from his left front foot and nailed him to the spot. Gasping, wild with pain and fear, he tried to free himself. But his foot was held fast in a terrible grip. Yelps of pain were dragged from him each time he tried to move.

He sank for a few moments to the dead leaves.

Then he threw himself on this thing that held him prisoner. His teeth met only iron, and he knew he was helpless against this new enemy.

A vague memory flitted across his mind. He recalled the precautions his mother took when she approached an unmoving prey. His impatience with one of these roundabout approaches had earned him a beating. And

that beating had driven him out to make his way alone.

He lay a long while licking at the tip of his bleeding paw. Two toes were caught fast in the trap.

Tatie and Piet stopped to listen at the edge of the trees. All was silent, save for the shaking of the leaves.

Piet called, "Mascot."

A whimper answered.

"Oh, this is dreadful," murmured Tatie.

"This way, to the left," said Piet.

They pushed through the brush. A border of hazelnut trees ringed the spot. Whipped by the flexible branches, they advanced, bent over, their arms up before their faces.

"This way," said a calm voice up ahead.

They soon came out of the underbrush. A surprise awaited them. There in the clearing was a stout stick holding one of Piet's posters. In front of the poster stood Taillefer's master, holding Mascot tight in his arms.

"Is he hurt?" cried Tatie.

"Only in his pride," laughed the man, "and that's not serious. He wanted to play with my dog, but Taillefer received his friendly advances rather badly."

Seeing his masters, Mascot struggled to get free. Let loose, he ran to Piet, then to Tatie, then to his new friend, delighted to introduce them to each other.

Taillefer sat a little to the side.

The man doffed his felt hat. "Good day, madame. Hello there, young man."

"Good day," said Tatie briefly. "And what are you doing here? Don't you see it's a dangerous spot?"

"Indeed, yes," said the man. "And you may have noticed that I stand perfectly still amid the dangers. These warnings, on all the hazelnuts, were first seen by my dog, who came to tell me about them. But the clever jokers who placed the posters went a little too far. They don't convince me, I'm afraid."

"Don't convince you?" Tatie exclaimed.

"Why not?" asked Piet.

"It seemed very much to me like a trick, the old trick of guaranteeing that the author of these anonymous signs would be left in peace to gather all the nuts from all these trees."

"These signs are not anonymous," said Tatie. "We put them up. And we hadn't even noticed the nut trees."

"The dickens you say," exclaimed the man. "And have you really put traps around?"

"And do you really believe that we would scheme to steal these nuts?"

"Well, well," thought Piet, "there goes Tatie's temper. The Old Gentleman had better watch his step."

"The stupidity of a thought, madame, is its own full condemnation," answered the man with a courtly air of faked contrition.

Piet was beginning to enjoy this. "Tatie's finally found someone who can really talk her language."

"But if there are traps, what about them?" the Old Gentleman continued.

"These traps," said Tatie crossly, "are lost. My

nephew, who placed them in my behalf, seems unable to find them again. When we heard your dog bark, we hurried out here."

"In other words, you were coming to our rescue, though it meant you ran the risk of being caught yourselves."

"As you say," said Tatie shortly. "How I wish this nightmare were over with!"

The Old Gentleman turned to Piet. "Let's see now, were the traps equipped with a chain?"

"Yes, they were."

"And you fixed the chain to a tree?"

"Yes, to a big tree, rather like these, I think," Piet answered, pointing to a young beech tree with a light trunk.

"In a clearing?" asked the hunter.

Piet thought. "Yes, under some leaves."

"What color were the leaves?"

"White," he said after a moment, "yes, white on one side anyway."

"But there are no white leaves," said Tatie.

The man put up a hand. "An aspen," he said. "There aren't any aspens on this side. They're lower down. Let's go see."

"What about the posters?"

"The posters are here. But the danger is elsewhere, if the traps are really near an aspen grove."

"That's the last straw," said Tatie. "The posters were protecting nothing, after all."

"I fear not," said the man soberly.

Piet, feeling rather sick, followed them down and around the slope. After that it was easy. At the sight of the first aspen, Piet recognized the place where he'd hidden the traps.

"There they are," he said, "a little to the left."

"How did you manage to make such a mistake?" asked Tatie.

"It wouldn't be difficult," said the Old Gentleman. "The border of the wood is a ring of nut trees. He merely mixed up hazelnuts and beeches."

The first trap was soon found under some leaves. With the end of his cane the Old Gentleman set off the spring. The jaws slammed together.

"What a dreadful thing!" said Tatie.

"The second one is a little lower down," said Piet.

Just then Taillefer, who had been sniffing the ground, gave a sharp little cry.

"That's interesting," said the man. "A fox has been by here during the night. Down, Taillefer."

The dog obeyed. Tatie took Mascot by the collar.

The second trap was empty, too.

A magpie cried from a treetop and another answered.

The hunter lifted his head. "I shouldn't be surprised," he said, "if we find something's been happening."

Piet's heart began to pound.

The magpie's dialogue continued. A third magpie came and perched, with a cry, atop a birch tree.

The sound of wild thrashing came from among the leaves. Then came the cry of an animal and a noise of flight. Taillefer whined with excitement.

The magpies flew off.

It took only a glance for the drama to become sharply clear to them.

Dead leaves and dirt, torn up and scattered in all directions, showed the prisoner's desperate determination to get free. A shred of russet fur between the jaws of the trap was still bleeding.

The old hunter bent over the ugly instrument.

"Poor creature, he got out of there just in time," he said. "But it cost him two toes to do it."

"Do you think he'll live?" asked Piet, horrified.

"Oh yes, he'll live. But his tracks will be easy to identify. Anyone who sees them will recognize the trail of the one-toed fox."

VIII

Tatie was so relieved to be free of her nightmare that she could have danced for joy. She asked the Old Gentleman to come back to the house with them.

Taillefer was whimpering with impatience, crouched obediently in the grass only twenty feet from the first bushes. Mascot broke free of Tatie's grasp and, at that, Taillefer gave a distressed cry. His master gestured to him to go, too. Joyously, he sped after the little white dog.

Because he had been so poorly treated by his new friend before, Mascot thought Taillefer was chasing him. He headed for Lina and the twins for protection.

The twins saw the dark shape of the basset and cried, "A fox, a fox!"

Taillefer was so dumbfounded at being mistaken for a fox that he turned tail and returned to his master.

How they all laughed! The children ran up to meet the Old Gentleman, then went down the hill in a cluster around Tatie.

Piet followed, the metal traps cling-clanging over his shoulder, dragging his feet like a slave in chains.

When the Old Gentleman saw the poultry yard sparkling in the sun with its new white clapboard and shining fences, he stopped, leaned on his cane, and looked at it from every angle.

Tatie expected a compliment.

She got one, though not quite what she'd expected.

"What a splendid toy!" said the Old Gentleman in a most elegant tone. "And are those tiny things real live chickens? Indeed they are; they're moving."

The children, not sure what to make of this, turned to Tatie.

"A very expensive toy," she said, "especially when foxes decide they'd like to play with it."

"Yes. And yet one must admit that they'd surely find it an irresistible temptation to have a poultry yard here. It's right out in the woods really. If I myself were a fox, I'm sure I'd never resist considering this as a convenient restaurant."

Lina giggled and led the twins toward the house. Piet, with his tinkling traps, followed.

"Is that the man you met the other day?" asked Lina.

"Yes, and he's terrific. He saved my life. And does he ever know things—all kinds of adventures and stories."

Piet told her about the crimson viper and the monkey.

"Don't let Tatie hear about the viper," advised Piet. "She mightn't let us go into the woods any more."

The children stood lined up on the little bridge over the water lock to await the arrival of their guest. It was a fine chance to get a good close look at this extraordinary person.

As he came along, he was talking gaily. Tatie was laughing hard.

"He must be telling a good one," said Gerard hopefully.

When the visitor came around the bend where he could see the house, he was suddenly quiet, as if struck by what he saw. At that hour the old mill showed itself in its best light. Under the blazing sun the golden stones took on a rosy glow, and the rich growth of ivy sparkled with thousands of drops of dew. The dark foliage of the maple gleamed doubly, mirrored in the calm sky-stained water.

As the Old Gentleman came into the main room, he seemed to radiate approval of the way it was arranged, with its profusion of leafy branches in huge earthenware jars.

The children were waiting, but not a story did they hear. Tatie carried the conversation alone. The Old Gentleman seemed almost in a hurry to be gone. He wasn't paying much attention to Tatie.

"Isn't he rude?" whispered Lina to her brother.

Just then, the Old Gentleman broke his silence. He cleared his throat and said, "You've made this into a perfectly charming place to live."

Tatie smiled a sociable smile.

"It would be even more charming if it weren't for the old monster," blurted Lina.

"Oh?" the visitor replied. "And who is this dreadful person?"

Tatie was making little warning signals. But Lina paid no heed.

"The landlord, of course," she cried. "He's a real monster. He pesters Tatie for money all the time."

"And he's going to tell us we're spoiling his house," added Gerard.

The Old Gentleman had the broadest smile they'd seen yet as he looked around the room.

"It's true that the place is old," he said.

"Yes, it's ready to fall apart. Tatie's fixed it up a lot, though," said Genevieve.

"You don't like it, then?" he asked.

"Oh, yes, we do; we love it," they all answered at once. "But if only Tatie didn't have so many things to worry about!"

The Old Gentleman, still smiling, said to Tatie, "You have a very devoted band of followers."

"I'm most terribly sorry," she murmured, her face scarlet and her bright eyes troubled.

The children stared. A mystery was in the air.

The Old Gentleman raised his hand. "Children, we might as well get this much clear at once. I am that old monster, your landlord."

"Ouch!" cried Lina. She didn't know how to hide her embarrassment. The twins opened wide eyes.

But the Old Gentleman seemed to find it very funny. "Don't be troubled." He laughed. "I think embarrassing moments always do more good than harm. This one makes me think of a story.

"My good friend, Elias Cabestan, was at one time fabulously wealthy. He had a palace in Lahore, to which he invited a minor maharaja for dinner. During the meal, Elias (who, like all good storytellers, has a wicked tongue) repeated a tale he'd heard a few days before. It was about one of the northern chiefs who had betrayed himself as a coward during a tiger hunt. It had become the joke of the year all over the region.

"When Elias had done, the maharaja only laughed

politely. Disappointed, Elias asked, 'You've heard the story before?'

" 'Yes,' said the prince, 'and I know that northern chief well. I am he.'

"There was a moment of dead silence, like the one we just had here."

Lina asked, "And then what happened?"

"Then the prince spoke again. 'Some time I'll tell you why I avoided that tiger. But I'd like to reassure you at once that it wasn't out of cowardice.' He drew a dagger, put his left hand on the table, and before Elias could stop him, he nailed his hand to the table with the dagger's sharp blade."

The children gasped.

"Wait, that's not all. As soon as Elias got over the shock, he seized his own dagger and in his turn nailed his own left hand to the table."

There was a horrified silence.

"Of course, it's not a true story?" said Tatie, trying to lighten the atmosphere.

"With Elias, it would be impossible to be sure," said the Old Gentleman.

The children were still staring at him with awe. They'd hoped he'd tell them a story, and they certainly had heard one.

Piet mused. "I wonder just what that story means?"

"Ah, there's the question," said the gentleman as if he'd expected it.

"I'll tell you. I admit I myself am quite incapable of such mock heroics. But insofar as this little affair of ours goes, I am the maharaja, and I nail my hand to the table."

"Nnnooo," wailed Genevieve.

Everyone laughed.

"No," said the man. "But I do plead guilty, and I must make a solemn gesture of some kind."

He gestured widely about the room and said, "The house is yours. I hereby give it to you free and clear."

"Oh no, you can't do that," Piet and Tatie cried.

"Yes, I can, easily. And now it's your turn to nail your hand to the table."

"What must we do?" asked Lina.

"Accept my gift, just like that, without protest. It'll be punishment enough for you."

There was a long dead silence. The children watched Tatie who sat full of emotion gazing at her clasped, capable hands.

"Sir," she said after a moment, "the children have put me in an impossible situation. Please don't take advantage of it."

"I admit I'm taking advantage. But if you could only know how happy it makes me, you'd say no more about it. One day I'll tell you children the story of this house, and you'll understand how wonderful it is for me to be able to give it to you."

"Couldn't you tell us now?" asked Piet.

"I'd rather not. It's only a very little story, but I need time to remember it properly."

His whole face was smiling now, as he looked around at the big-eyed children.

"Taillefer, my friend, have you had enough rest?"

"Yap," said Taillefer, smiling so wide his back teeth showed.

"Then we'll take our leave. Say good-by for now to everyone."

"I'll come with you as far as the hill," said Tatie.

Toward the end of the day, Bigson came into the dark woods of the high plateau, in the very depths of the forest. His whole body was one solid ache. The pain had spread into all his muscles. He went on, deaf and blind, driven by an instinct from the scene of his disaster. The fire in his torn paw had turned into an enormous weight that he dragged like an iron ball.

From time to time the wound struck a log or a stone. That would make him whimper aloud and hurry on his limping course. He had to go farther still, and keep going, as if he hoped to leave the pain behind.

Along his passage the animals kept quiet. He moved, followed by a long wake of silence through the forest. Only an occasional sarcastic cry came from a magpie or jay in their scrapey, rusted voices.

Bigson didn't hear them. He noticed only the buzzing of his fever; of all the forest, he saw only shapes, either dark or lighter masses, as if he walked in a dense fog.

He took a long drink from a brook at the foot of a ravine. It made him feel better, and then he decided to stay close to the brook. He went upstream along its bank. It led him to the pinewoods that covered the slopes around the High Place at the heart of the forest.

Completely spent, he flattened out in a sort of nook by an old uprooted tree stump next to a rock. He'd reached the end of his strength. He knew at last that he couldn't run away from his pain.

He lay on his flank, panting. He looked at the night, the twisted rock forms, the logs all around him. Above him the black branches were so close that he couldn't see the sky. Where his foot rested on the earth, he had the impression that the earth itself shuddered. Gently, he began to lick the wound, and each touch of his tongue made a spur of pain shoot through his whole body.

It was violent, but this self-provoked pain helped to quiet his anguish. It seemed to him that he became, little by little, the master of his own destiny once more.

For several days the hurt fox lay almost motionless in his earthy nook. His only neighbors were a sickly stag, so old that his fur seemed covered with gray moss, and a hairy, humpbacked wild pig who looked as thought he were pushing an enormous snout from which came a perpetual groaning snore.

Bigson grew thinner. His spirits were low. The September nights were humid and cold. Each morning, the front of his nook was covered with dew-drenched spider webs that glinted in the rising sun. It almost seemed that the spiders thought they could shut the fox up into his place of refuge. It was through their sparkling veiling that Bigson's two neighbors peered to see if he were still alive each morning.

As luck had it, he was still alive. His young flesh rapidly formed a scar. But the wound reopened when, driven by thirst, he got up and went to drink at the brook. This weakened him and made his convalescence longer.

However, day by day, the skin puckered and grew thicker. The paw was less painful, and he could put it to earth. Fever finally stopped burning in his thin body. Then Bigson felt hunger return. One fine morning, he broke through the spider webs over his door and set out on the hunt.

When his two neighbors came to see how he was, they found his nook empty.

IX

The Commandant came several times to the mill with
Taillefer. And after Lina's unforgettable blunder, the
children were careful of what they said. Piet had threat-
ened to beat the gizzard out of the first one to mention
the house. At first Tatie was on hot coals when the Old
Gentleman was there.

However, she grew calmer as the children proved
they were capable of mannerly behavior. School would
reopen soon. It was time to see what to do next.

A good many letters were exchanged between the
children's parents and Tatie. After much discussion it
was decided that the children should stay a while longer
with their aunt. The twins would go to the village
school; Piet and Lina would go each day to the
Fontenay high school. With that decided, they could
enjoy waiting for school to start.

Tatie and the children took advantage of the last fine
days. They were out of doors most of the time. Their
evening walks along the brook told them the days were
shorter, for the September stars shone innumerable. The
Milky Way, above the hills, traced its vaporous path-

way, disappearing behind the trees around the High Place at the head of the forest.

One evening as they strolled along, a sleepy voice said, "Tatie, has the Commandant told you the story of the house?"

Piet gave a stifled groan. Lina coughed. Tatie didn't answer at once.

"Yes," she admitted after a minute. "I know the story of the house." She was silent a bit before going on. "It's a sad story, you see, and you mayn't understand it very well."

"I love sad stories," said Lina. "But you can change the ending around if you want."

"Well, then, you may perhaps be able to change the ending of this one. Who knows? Here's the story."

"When the Old Gentleman was your age, he was a sickly child and often had to stay in bed. He lived in his parents' house. It was lonely because his parents were old, and the servants were too. He had no playmates at

all. Their house was in the forest, near the source of this very brook, I understand. It's a sort of chateau, near a pond."

"Is this story true?" asked Genevieve.

"Quite true."

"Is the chateau still there?"

"Of course. Well, the little boy liked to go walking alone in the forest. One day he discovered our old mill. That day, it was raining, and the boy needed to take shelter. He managed to get into the mill by the little back window.

"He explored all the rooms. He soon decided it would be fun to fix them up to suit himself.

"He came every day after that. He made a fire on the hearth and spent long hours by himself. One afternoon he fell asleep and didn't get home until after dark. His parents had been so worried that they had sent search parties for him through the forest. After that he told them about his secret hiding place and asked for permission to spend his time there. His parents agreed and had it fixed up for him. He was about fifteen then. One day a group of boys and girls, who were spending their

vacation on the other side of the forest, stopped at the mill. They had lost their way in the woods. They thought the owner of the mill might give them a place to rest and directions for returning home. They were completely amazed when they saw a boy their own age living there all alone, proprietor of the mill. He invited them in and explained. Before they left, they said they'd like to come back to visit him.

"This is the part that's hard to explain," said Tatie. "You children have never been lonely, so you'll just have to take my word for it that the boy was overwhelmed with joy to have found friends. He was happy, really happy for the first time. Happier than you can imagine.

"His guests returned, as they had promised, and soon they were a sort of family at the mill—a family of young people. It only lasted for the weeks of summer vacation. But all year long the boy thought of his friends. They wrote each other and made plans for the next summer. He lived in the thought of their return.

"Things went on this way for several years until the young people were in their twenties.

"And then came their last holidays, in the month of July, 1914."

"Nineteen fourteen!" cried Lina. "Did it happen so long ago?"

Piet said, "World War I began in that year, 1914. I know what happened; the boys had to go off to war."

"Yes, the boys went to war. Before they went, they promised to come back to the mill the next summer.

They thought the war would surely be over by then.

"It was, instead, a long and terrible war. Not one of the boys ever returned."

"And the girls?"

"The girls didn't come back either. They got married near their own homes, far from here. They're old ladies now."

"And the boy who was all alone?"

"He too had intended to take up his old life here again when he returned. But he couldn't bear to be so lonely where he'd once had companions. He left again, this time on a boat. He sailed all the world's seas."

"Is that why he's called Commandant?"

"Yes, I suppose it is. Well, he came back for good finally when he was old. And he found himself alone again, perhaps even more alone than when he'd been a child. He lives with his dog in the chateau, where his parents once lived, and spends his time in the forest.

"Mr. Becu is in complete charge of his business affairs. He didn't even know the mill had been rented to strangers."

"You know, I noticed he was surprised that first day when I said we were staying at the mill. Now I know why," cried Piet.

"And to think that I called him an old monster," murmured Lina.

"And has he really given us the house for keeps?" asked Gerard.

"I told you kids to hush," growled Piet.

They all turned to Tatie. It was obvious that she wouldn't answer. She looked both knowing and embarrassed.

For Bigson, that autumn had the vigor and excitement of springtime. His hard times were over. He'd gained both strength and confidence. He went marauding wherever he chose, trying his wits against clever old foxes. These veterans were jealous of their kingdoms. Bigson gave them something to worry about, stealing a rabbit or two occasionally from the warrens they had staked out for themselves and watched so jealously.

His enforced rest seemed to have given him an extra measure of vitality. He didn't limp. His movements were as supple as ever. Only his tracks revealed his injury. The print of his left foot looked like a mutilated flower from which two petals out of three were missing. The scar was still rather sensitive, and he preferred to avoid pebbly or rocky soil when possible. Also, any large digging project was out of the question.

These difficulties, small in themselves, made Bigson reflective and careful. He had to make up for the physical handicap he'd suffered by using all his wits all the time. He'd had several warnings against carelessness. The lessons of his mother, that wise old vixen, came back to him as if by magic. And now he was determined to make good use of them. His painful adventure gave him wisdom and acuteness beyond his years. He could measure himself against any of the older denizens of the forest.

Since the day he had left his dark refuge on the High Place, he had done little but eat and sleep. He would eat anything as long as there was enough of it, and sleep anywhere provided it was dry and quiet. He had charged out of a thousand different hiding places, sowing fear and disquiet among the deer as well as the rabbits, on the leafy high ground as well as along the borders of the plain and even in the farmyards. The more placid part of the forest's population had the impression that the dread race of foxes had suddenly increased enormously.

Finally, though, Bigson's enormous hunger was satisfied. Its place was taken by a growing need to own a domain all his own, one he in his turn could proudly defend against intruders. The October rains forced him to take refuge in whatever holes he happened to find. But as soon as the days were fair again he started to look for his future kingdom.

It was hunting season. The plain and the woods were overrun with dogs of all shapes and sizes. Shots rang out and were multiplied by the echoes. From dawn to dark the inhabitants of the woods were on the alert. The tracks of hunted creatures crossed and recrossed, making a whole network of inescapable terror from one end to the other of the forest floor.

Animals were done to death every day. Others, mortally wounded, dragged their hurt bodies off and hid themselves to die. Some little bands of animals, chased from spot to spot, had no rest except at night. The wild pigs went up into the deepest part of the woods and stayed there, under the black bushes. The rabbits lay flat in their holes, transfixed with fear. Even the foxes and the badgers did not dare to go far from their strongholds.

Bigson followed the events with his usual attention. He soon understood that, lacking a sure place of refuge, his best defense was to keep moving.

At dawn, he went up to a height where he could overlook the neighborhood. At that season the hunters paid little attention to the foxes, whose fur was still sparse and of small value. Bigson was safe enough. He had only to stay out of sight lest he attract the attention of some novice hunter who might use him as target for a practice shot. If by chance the dogs came too close, he knew he would have to find a way out before the gunners could encircle him.

Flattened under the brush, he listened to the barking dogs and the echoing rifle shots. Sometimes his ease was troubled only by the noise, and he dozed, his eyes half closed, in the welcome warmth of a late-season afternoon.

If the sounds of the hunt reached the nearby valleys, he quietly made for some other, more tranquil height.

At night he rapidly toured the hunting grounds. He had no trouble picking up wounded animals or stupid ones who were too glad to have escaped the afternoon's slaughter to keep up their guard at night. However, he still had no place of his own. From height to height he was pushed back, until he came one day to the High Place, which he had not visited since his convalescence.

The landscape looked less severe than the last time he had seen it. He circled back and forth over it. Here he could establish a wonderful kingdom. True, game was not very plentiful. But he could extend his reach almost indefinitely. There was no other fox in the vicinity; he would have no competition. The old stag and the wild pig would not be in his way. The brook would provide drinking water, even in midsummer. And since he would be at the forest's highest point, he could raid downward in all directions from a position of strength. A careful study of the countryside confirmed his decision. He would become the Master of the High Place.

He made the nook between a tree stump and a rock into his temporary refuge. Then he got busy marking the frontiers of his territory.

He chose a dry, cold morning. A light white frost glazed the edge of the flatland within the pinewood. Dawn had just begun to redden the earth.

Standing outside his nook, Bigson sniffed the wind, then went down toward the brook. It would be through this valley that most visitors might be expected to come. Bigson wanted to warn them that after a certain point they would be entering a private domain.

He chose a spur of rock that barred off almost the entire width of the valley. Rain and wind had swept it clear of moss and vegetation, so that the surface was bare and clean.

There on that promontory, Bigson left healthy-sized droppings. This signal would be understood by the entire forest population. He marked the place as his. It would be enough for him to come and renew his signal from time to time.

That duty done, he crossed the valley and walked in a wide circle around the summit of the High Place.

Here and there he left his marks of ownership. He urinated against a log, against a rocky rise; he rubbed against the trunk of an oak or a beech; he managed to leave a little of his scent behind wherever he halted.

It was an interesting walk. He found a medlar tree whose fruit, softened by the cold snap, lay scattered on the ground. Pleased by this new dessert, he promised himself to return for snacks of fruit before long. He saw several animal carcasses. They told him that the High Place had often served as a last refuge for hurt or sick animals who instinctively sought out a calm spot to finish their days.

Bigson found every reason to be glad he'd decided to take over the High Place. He would reign royally here and, in time of need, would be able to raid his neighbors' domains, or even the flatland farms.

For several days he walked that same circle, exploring his territory and finding new reasons to rejoice in it. The borders he had set seemed to be respected. He found no need, just now, to bother deer that trooped up into his woods. He hoped, some day, to take by surprise some fawn lost or separated from the herd. He delighted in his wealth and lordship over a proud kingdom.

All at once, however, this fine dream of security collapsed. One evening as Bigson was returning to his nook, his stomach full and his heart light, he came abruptly on a creature he had never met in his neighborhood before. It was a low-slung fellow, short-legged but solidly built and well set. His grayed fur was light along the flanks, and his white head bore two black bands on either side of his muzzle. He was a powerful-looking badger.

Bigson stopped, holding his breath. The badger hadn't noticed him. He was strolling along, perfectly calm. His self-confident air annoyed Bigson. This intruder apparently felt right at home here.

Bigson's first impulse was to jump him. But he looked again at the badger's imposing muscles and decided the encounter might present problems. He satisfied himself with merely following the big fellow, ready to attack if he had to.

He didn't have to. The animal was an old hand. He led Bigson on a long walk that included most of the domain Bigson had marked out as his own. The badger paid no heed to the fox's proprietary warnings but wandered all night and went to his own home again at dawn. Bigson followed him. He saw him proceed slowly into his lair that lay a little upstream from the source of the brook.

When the badger had gone to earth, the fox examined the spot. He had to admit that it was extremely well placed. He examined its various entrances, noting how clean and well kept they were. There could be no objection to its site; there'd be no fear of flooding here. Neither rain nor wind would penetrate this house.

Full of envy, jealousy, and anger, the fox went

around the lair several times. He could tell that its owner had been there for a long time and had made every possible arrangement for leading a comfortable existence.

Bigson thought of his own miserable nook. It was a poor vagabond's corner open to every wind. He wondered what to do. His pride was hurt. Should he look elsewhere for a kingdom? Would he try battle to the death to gain this one?

The badger couldn't possibly ignore Bigson's arrival in his territory. Why hadn't he shown himself? Would he swallow the idea of sharing his authority? Or worst of all, did he think the young fox too insignificant to bother with? Bigson was determined to find out.

He thought for a minute. Then he went, majestically, up to the main entrance of the lair. There, right in the middle of the sill, he deposited a large dropping.

It was his declaration of war.

Bigson lay flat in the shadow of a dense juniper bush and waited for the badger to come out. It was a beautiful mid-October evening. The wind blew from the east, dry and cold, but the sun had warmed the woods and the exposed slopes. The earth kept its warmth under its cover of leaves and brush. It was delicious weather. Toward the west, the heavens turned softly lilac.

The old stag and then the old wild pig came by, a few seconds after each other, going toward the thick cover of the High Place. Bigson greeted them with a short, light bark, but they didn't hear him and went on their way.

The clearing was shaped like an amphitheater. Its gentle slope was marked with a hole, the entrance to the badger's lair.

Bigson kept his eyes fixed on the hole. He wanted to watch his adversary's first reaction to his challenge. He hoped that the enemy would be irritated enough to return the challenge. Bigson wasn't sure whether he'd accept it right away. Everything depended on circumstances. In any case, he'd keep the advantage of surprise for himself.

He felt strong. He rather looked forward to the idea of a good fight. But the badger was a powerful enemy, whom it would be foolish to underestimate.

Bigson had a surprise coming. Nothing happened as he had expected.

A low growling advised him that his challenge had been noticed. The badger peered out of the hole but drew his head in again at once. A few seconds later Bigson saw the white-splotched head again and heard the badger begin a series of complaints. They weren't angry ones but, instead, were the distressed sounds of a neat homeowner who finds that sloppy neighbors have dirtied the land around his house.

"Ha roum, roum, ha roum roum," the badger muttered, pacing up and down. He seemed to be looking all over, not for an enemy, but for an instrument to sweep his doorstep clean.

Finally, with the tip of his claws, he rolled Bigson's dropping away, pushing it as if with a broom as far as possible from the entrance. Then he rapidly dug a hole and dumped the thing in, covering it with earth. Next he neatly trampled the ground smooth and made a brief tour of inspection to make sure there were no other dirty tokens about. At last, satisfied, he went off at a short trot.

Bigson hadn't made a sound. He had learned a lot from this scene. The badger wasn't going to be provoked into a battle. And a thought slipped into his mind. Why risk a fight when it mightn't be necessary?

The badger's house was probably extremely comfortable. Bigson, with his hurt paw, couldn't expect to dig too far or too well, so why not take up residence in the badger's house, simply, just like that? The badger could easily find or dig another home. He had sturdy claws, well adapted to digging, and powerful muscles.

Bigson didn't wait. He acted on his impulse at once. In one bound he had left his hiding place and gone toward the entrance to the lair.

The interior was, as he had hoped, big and very comfortable. There were several communicating rooms. The last, dug deep, had a sort of emergency exit that came out almost at the edge of the woods. You couldn't imagine a better dwelling place.

Bigson filled the lair with his personal smell. The badger couldn't help but know that a fox had installed himself in the house while he was out.

Time would tell how he'd react to that.

A little before daybreak, Bigson went on a short hunting expedition. He came back soon. He didn't want to miss the return of the badger.

He had a long wait outside the lair. Nothing happened, even when the forest stirred and woke in the silence and stillness of a cold day. The sky was an infinity of purest light.

Bigson was distracted for a moment by the arrival of a blackbird who had come to nibble at the juniper bush. Yellow-Beak stood pecking among the grasses only a foot away. The fox pulled himself into a crouch, his eye keen, his nose pointed. Just as he was about to leap, he saw something emerge from the woods. There came not one, but two, white-marked heads. As Bigson turned to look, the blackbird flew off with a cry of fright.

Bigson didn't care about the bird now. There stood the two badgers chatting in front of their lair. Bigson knew his neighbor by his imposing size. The other was smaller—his wife, probably. So he was really up against two enemies. Things didn't look too good. He decided to lie still awhile and think this out.

The lady of the house went in first. She got half her body down the hole and came out again quickly, disgusted by the smell. The two white heads looked all around the clearing. Their short-sighted eyes gave them only a dim and uncertain view of the surroundings. Bigson saw them tilt their heads and shake their muzzles. Both seemed quite embarrassed. What a business! What a stink!

"Kaou kaou," barked Bigson, fairly loud.

The badgers ducked down their hole fast.

A big smile lit up the fox's face. It looked as though he'd win without a fight after all. He was almost sure

now. These poor folk weren't at all warlike. He'd only have to insist a little to take his place in their lair.

Three days later, the matter was settled. The two badgers hadn't lost their dignity in quarreling. They had simply dug out new apartments, adjoining their old ones, which they left for Bigson. They contented themselves with opening a special above-ground entrance giving directly on to their rooms, in this new two-family lair.

This victory, won without a blow, filled Bigson with pride and joy. Now he was truly a lord of the land. His neighbors were silent and polite. They kept the lair and its surroundings in a state of meticulous cleanliness. They would even tidy away the remains of game that

Bigson left near his doorway when he'd finished with it.

Eventually, the pleasure of newness wore off. Bigson's right to his domain and his chosen home was clearly established.

Then Bigson began that series of long raids, which made him famous over all the Mervent country.

X

After a few days of windy cold, the weather grew soft again. There were long, warm evenings, like the fairest ones of summer.

Over the plain the farmers were hurrying to get in the last of their harvest. The grape-gathering was over. Evenings, voices of men working over the grapes rose from the cellars. Lights burned late behind the low little windows crisscrossed with spider webs. Confused by the mild air into thinking summer had really returned, the farm creatures stayed late outside the barns.

Bigson pulled off several poultry massacres. When the farmers dashed out of the stables at the sound of squawks and screams, they saw only a flourish of feathers and the flight of an animal over the stile.

Word soon got around that an enormous and amazingly daring fox was devastating the countryside's chicken yards. People claimed to have seen him everywhere at once. His growing exploits exasperated villagers for miles round about.

One evening Piet had gone for milk to the neighboring farm. Cries rang out in the courtyard, "Get that fox!

Get him, get him!" The chickens were squawking. The farm hands ran in all directions with raised pitchforks.

This time the adventure almost had a sad ending for the thief. Dogs ran on one side, farm hands on the other. The ways out were blocked.

Seeing his retreat cut off, Bigson dashed across the courtyard. In one unbelievable leap he crossed the pool that was used as a barnyard drinking place. Luckily for him, at this season the water was low. He landed on the muddy bank and ran for the fields. The farmer came out of the barn with a lantern. "That's no fox," he cried. "It's a wolf. Foxes never take leaps like that."

The farm hands assured him that it was indeed a fox. Going round the greenish ditch, the men went to look over the thief's tracks. Piet followed.

"These tracks don't belong to any fox," cried the farmer. "Look here."

They all bent over the tracks. They saw, clearly imprinted, the mark of a paw.

"Whatever the creature is, he has only one toe!"

The men looked at each other. They had never seen a one-toed beast.

"But I'm sure it was a fox. I saw his tail," said one.

"And look here! You can see, here's a clear fox track."

"But then what about that one-toed paw print?"

"He's just a one-armed bandit! Old One-Toe!" laughed the farmer.

Piet looked at the peculiar print and said not a word. He recalled the Commandant's words, "Everyone will call him the one-toed fox."

Well, there it was. Piet had seen his victim once more. The print was of a left foot. There could be no doubt it was the same fox, the one they'd caught in the trap.

Some days later, he saw that fox track again.

That night Bigson had had a strange feast in a little wood not far from the plain. There he had discovered a cluster of young turkeys who had acquired the habit of sleeping in the lower branches of a cedar tree. The clump of cedars was part of a park surrounded by a wall that was topped by a grating. The creatures must have thought themselves safe. But the wall had fallen in at one point, and Bigson had no trouble getting in.

He looked over the park. In the distance he could see the front of a house half hidden by trees. The night wasn't very dark. Toward the east the lower part of the sky was tinged with rose. The moon would soon rise.

Emboldened by his series of victories, he went forward with his supple gait, scraping past the trimmed bushes and the tufts of light-plumed reeds.

He suddenly heard a series of sleepy cluckings. He stopped short and listened. Sniffing the breeze, he learned that the sounds were coming from the little woods nearby.

He ran over lawns toward the cedar trees. Overhead against the sky he could see the sleeping fowl. They were big black outlandish creatures, balancing on the horizontal branches. Were they really asleep? At any rate, they weren't moving. From time to time one of them clucked a bit, another shifted his weight, swaying as if about to fall.

The fox's mouth filled with saliva.

How could he get at them? He went back and forth below the tree, his head lifted toward this stupid but inaccessible game.

He tried a few leaps, stretching up along the tree trunk, but it was no good.

He'd been there several minutes, when the moon showed herself at the edge of the sky, enormous and copper-red. The landscape was adazzle with light. Glittering dew covered the lawns with tracks of brilliance. The fowl shifted on their perch.

At the end of his patience, Bigson made two or three leaps, his muzzle lifted skyward.

At his last leap, with his nose only a few inches away from his prey, he could make out one of the turkey's heads bent toward him. The bird was staring at him with fixed round eyes, as if petrified.

The fox whimpered with rage. Again he leaped, his jaws open. He fell back and leaped again, tense as a spring. A dozen times he tried and failed. Out of breath, he panted with exhaustion and fury.

Suddenly, without any warning, the turkey he'd been snatching at fell like an overripe fruit. Bigson couldn't believe his eyes. But there the creature was, between his paws, tender and tasty as anyone could dream.

When he'd eaten a few mouthfuls, he lifted his head. The other turkeys were watching, as if the fate of their companion had nothing to do with them.

He was too much of a fox to let one turkey be enough. Just to see if it could happen again, Bigson tried his leaping dance once more. He had scarcely made four leaps when a second, then a third turkey dropped to his strong teeth. He rapidly settled their fate and began all over again.

All the fowl fell eventually, hypnotized by his dance. It was incredible. Stuffed with meat, Bigson didn't even bother to drag off the leftovers to be hidden for the future. Why save up provisions, when it was so easy to pick up all he needed whenever he chose?

Gone were the days when as a young, inexperienced fox he'd run hither and yon, bedeviled by hunger. He'd come a long way since then. Already he was master of this country, and it spread riches generously before him.

Though it wasn't yet midnight, Bigson had already finished hunting. He went slowly away from the slaughter, happy to breathe the gentle air full of forest freshness.

He looked up toward the High Place, but he wasn't sleepy. Before returning to his lair, he wanted to walk around a little and digest his meal. Truth to tell, he felt rather heavy. A walk would do him good.

At the edge of a field of grain, he saw a pair of rabbits who noticed his shadow and ran off in a wild leap. Poor devils, always trembling with terror! Bigson wished them no harm—tonight, at least.

A little farther on he saw a family of wild pigs busily digging in the earth, looking for potatoes the farmer had forgotten. As Bigson passed, an old male turned his head and growled.

Bigson began to bark in his sharp voice. It frightened a covey of partridge and sent them flying up from the grass. He felt the watchfulness of all the animals of the night. The fear his presence wakened made his pride increase.

Only when the moon had begun to dip down behind the other rim of the horizon did he think of going back to his domain. At that point, he passed not far from the farm where the children went each evening to get milk.

He knew this farm well from having stolen chickens there. This time he had no clear idea of what he wanted to do. However, he went close. It was then that he smelled a strange scent, at once bitter and sugary.

He stopped, sniffing the air on all sides.

The smell was really delicious. Bigson felt his mouth moisten. He'd like to locate this delectable sweet. Peering right and left, he finally came up to a low building. Before it were piled enormous brown cakes of pressed grapes from the wine-making.

Delicately nipping with his teeth, Bigson tasted the warm sweetness. He found it a little dry but full of savour and delectably perfumed. He pushed a big hole in one of the cakes and found that the inside was much more tender and not at all dry. He bit out big mouthfuls. Soon a strange warmth enveloped him. He suddenly felt himself extraordinarily joyous and full of life, as if each mouthful doubled his strength and his courage. Pushing his muzzle into the scented cake up to the eyes, he felt this special gaiety growing in him. He wanted to leap and gambol and climb trees and do a million silly things.

Finally he went off dancing like a young goat, barking at his shadow, calling to the moon that seemed to topple out of the sky, sending out calls to all sides. The echoes repeated his nonsense round the woods.

In that state he arrived at Tatie's mill.

Mascot jumped awake and began barking insanely. Bigson answered him with insults. The house, the brook, the trees, all seemed tiny to him, and the furious barkings of a mere dog were so comical that they made him weep tears of joy. He'd never known such a feast day. He followed his road, still dancing, under the trees toward the High Place.

As he went, he called out to the owls who opened wide eyes at him from the doors of their holes. He invited the squirrels to come somersaulting among the briars. He made mad speeches to the rabbits, atremble with terror in their warrens. He let the whole forest know that an extraordinary adventure had happened to the Master of the High Place.

Having recognized their neighbor's voice, Lord and Lady Badger drew their white heads back quickly into their apartments. They observed the arrival of Bigson, staggering drunk in the moonlight. Scandalized, they retreated to their own quarters.

XI

Piet, wakened by Mascot's barking, ran to his window. What he saw filled him at first with something like fright.

On the embankment along the little pond, a strange beast gave himself over to a wild dance in the moonlight. The creature seemed unreal, its movements were so disordered and without meaning. It might have been a dance of joy, but it might equally well have been the madness of a creature tormented by dreadful agony.

Piet watched the spectacle, thinking of the tales of spooks he had heard at the farm. What if the fantastic animal that danced in the pale shifting moonlight were the Bloodless Beast who appeared over and over in the farmers' tales?

It took him a long moment to recognize the fox's silhouette. But then, he'd never heard of a fox acting so peculiarly. Of course, he couldn't know that Bigson was drunk, lightheaded and loaded with alcohol from the pressed grapes.

As soon as it was day, Piet ran out onto the embankment and recognized the tracks of the one-toed bandit.

His goings and comings, his disordered leaps, were written plain on the soft earth. It was only necessary to follow the prints to learn his path across the forest.

Piet decided this was an opportunity not to be missed. His natural history teacher had recently asked him to bring in some specimens of mushrooms to show the class. He'd collect those and kill two birds with one stone.

He had soon picked all the mushrooms he needed. The damp warmth of the last few days had made mushrooms of all shapes and colors spring out of the earth.

The mysterious life of these strange plants fascinated him. He had heard of poisonous varieties and delicious ones growing right next to each other, and so alike that they seem to have been made by some devilish force just to confuse hungry men.

He had talked about them with the Commandant. He was a real expert and had showed Piet how to recognize those rare species that really are dangerous.

"As for myself"—the Commandant had laughed—"the dangerous species aren't the poisonous ones. The delicious ones make trouble for me, because I'm very fond of them. If I eat as many as I like, I have indigestion afterward."

Piet made a selection of boleti, amanites, and chanterelles, along with some less well-known species that are of a shape very different from ordinary mushrooms.

He hid his harvest under a bush and set out on the trail of the fox.

He had no trouble in following One-Toe's path. But

the tracks wandered so far that he was afraid he must be mistaken. Several times he was tempted to give up the search.

"I must be following old tracks," he thought. "They won't lead me anywhere at all."

Yet when he looked closely, he saw that the tracks were all fresh and clearly marked.

Finally he reached the High Place and followed One-Toe's trail to the lair in the midst of its little clearing in the pinewood.

The happiness he found in this success made him forget how tired he was.

But then he began to wonder. What could he do with his discovery? He had no intention of capturing One-Toe. Ever since the sad adventure of the trap he had felt guilty. The life of the young fox was somehow precious to him. And yet he couldn't deny he'd found pleasure in tracking One-Toe down.

He began to laugh. "What a hunter!" he thought. "Hunting without a gun. I'm a silly idiot. Lucky nobody saw me."

His joy was doubled. He didn't care if he did seem silly. "Hunt without guns? And why not! Who's to stop me?"

All at once he glimpsed some of the limitless pleasure he might find in simply learning to know the creatures that intrigued him. He'd want nothing from them but the chance to learn how they lived.

He would follow their trails, watch over their walks and their games and the struggle they led for existence. He might even help them or come in as a discreet umpire of their conflicts.

From a distance he examined the entrance to the lair. Maybe One-Toe was lying flat behind its threshold, watching him mistrustfully. Hoping he hadn't frightened him unnecessarily, Piet went off without making any noise.

From that day on, Piet spent his free time in the forest. Soon he knew its hills and slopes and ravines as well as any of its inhabitants. The discovery enchanted him. He had once thought it impossible to distinguish one from another in the multitude of creatures that inhabit a forest. But very soon he saw that he met the same creatures in more or less the same places at about the same times each day. He came on a pack of deer at the drinking place, or foxes out hunting, or big lone stags or even wild pigs. He soon learned their favorite forest paths and their well-marked passages along the ridges of earth that bordered the ditches.

He even got to know the most secret denizens of the woods, the badgers and the others. But of course it was the foxes that interested him most, especially his friend, One-Toe.

It was an odd friendship. At first, when Bigson encountered this man-shape near his lair, he'd been worried by it. And after he had escaped a few rifle bullets elsewhere, he grew still more mistrustful. But he soon began to distinguish the hunter from the unarmed man. Tracked several times by farmers furious at his misdeeds, he'd grown expert at avoiding these fire bearers. He knew how to save himself by going through the side of a hunt where only spectators or beaters were stationed. He knew that the beaters, talkative and never still, weren't dangerous. On the other hand, he knew he must avoid the still, silent watchers who stood under cover along the forest passages.

Piet, because of his stillness and silence, was like the hunters who in one sudden gesture sent out their fatal fire. But he was of a special species so far as One-Toe could see. He didn't carry that long stick that sends out death across long distances.

Several times Piet had the satisfaction of seeing the fox go by not far from him without hastening his short trot, though the fox knew he was observed. That made Piet's joy complete. He knew that One-Toe recognized him without fearing him.

He'd gone a number of times to see the Commandant, and told him about his discoveries. The old man was delighted to see the lad take an interest in the inhabitants of the forest. They talked for hours and looked up things in books that confirmed Piet's own observations.

One thing, however, was never mentioned. Held back by an indescribable shyness, Piet never made clear his friendly feelings for One-Toe.

Some days later he congratulated himself on his discretion.

As the first cold set in, the farmers who lived near the forest found themselves with more free time. They took their guns, whistled up their dogs, and went out hunting. Sometimes Piet met them and had to put up with their jokes at his expense. Was he out racing hares? Was he catching pheasants with a pinch of salt for their tails? Was he hoping to lead home a fox on a piece of string?

Piet answered, laughing, that he had a secret.

"Maybe so," they'd answer. "Maybe the Commandant has shown you some of his secret tricks."

Piet learned from them that the Commandant was known as the most effective hunter in the land, especially in fox hunting. He'd caught innumerable foxes. People came from miles around to ask his help in destroying the sly russet thieves no one else could catch or kill.

This particular winter, the talk of the countryside was the exploits of a certain one-toed bandit whose telltale prints had been seen everywhere. Expert old hunters dreamed of tracking him down. Everyone secretly set out to hunt with the hope of being the first to succeed in killing him. It would mean carrying off the honors of the season.

That was why Piet met a good many hunters out alone, with furtive, serious faces, silent men with guns, who were frightening to see. Piet thought they looked like assassins.

The sight of the young boy was far from pleasing to them. But Piet knew that the best way to save his friend's life, if One-Toe were indeed nearby, was to engage the hunter in talk.

"Hello there," he'd cry. "Looking for One-Toe?"

The men would shrug their shoulders. "You know, there's too much fancy talk about this One-Toe. He's just an animal like the rest. No more, no less. I'm not after him. I want to bring back some magpies to put up over my seed bed at the end of a stick. The messy things do a lot of damage at my place."

That was the favorite excuse. Piet didn't believe a word of it. These old experts liked to surround their affairs with mystery. He knew that this time, at least, the game wouldn't be played to a fatal finish. If the fox had been around, he'd have been warned off by the sound of voices. He'd not be taken by surprise.

Once Piet had got the hunter's attention, he'd ask about other foxes and hunts in other years. The hunter would begin to expand. In answering Piet's questions by telling some extraordinary hunting and shooting story, he'd forget to resent being interrupted.

One Thursday afternoon, Piet found himself at the Commandant's house. It had started to storm while he was in the forest, and he'd taken refuge at the chateau.

Delighted by his visit, the old man had welcomed him into the library.

The arrival of a car interrupted their talk. Madame TaHo, the housekeeper, brought the visitors in, and the Commandant welcomed them as old friends.

From what Piet understood, they were the owners of neighboring properties. They had met together at the home of one of them to arrange for a hunting party. Piet grew tense at once and listened hard. It was clear that this was to be no ordinary hunt. They were most anxious for the Commandant to come. Their eagerness meant that the quarry must be a formidable one. Piet was sure that sooner or later they'd say the name of One-Toe.

The hunters began by making fun of the rumors that were going the rounds of the villages and farms. There was talk of a mysterious beast whose paws had only one toe. There was even talk of sorcery and magic. These men knew, of course, that it was only a fox.

"I know something about it," said one of the proprietors. "He strangled twelve turkeys in my park not three weeks ago."

"It's a very intelligent animal," said another. "A few clumsy hunters have had a shot at it, and it's grown very wary, very cunning."

The conversation continued for several minutes. Piet watched the Commandant. He let the neighbors talk, approving, nodding his head. Piet was sure the Commandant knew better than they what animal they meant. When someone said the creature bore the mark of an injury to its left foot, the Old Gentleman turned toward Piet and said, with a wink, "Then all this is about our wily old friend."

"Do you know him, too?" the others exclaimed.

"This young man took him in a trap, near the mill."

Piet at once became an important person. He was surrounded. How had he gone about it? What bait had he used? How had the trap been hidden? How very interesting! And of course he'd have to take part in the hunt.

Piet agreed. He had his own ideas about what part he'd take. The surest way to help One-Toe was to be present in the ranks of his enemies.

It was decided that the Commandant should be in charge of the arrangements. He'd study the fox's behavior and on a suitable day he'd summon the hunters. They'd follow whatever plan of attack he recommended.

Piet went back to the mill, his face hot with excitement, his heart troubled. That evening, he told Lina and the twins all about the situation. He told about his walks in the forest, his meetings with One-Toe, and his friendliness toward this animal whose injury was their fault.

Tatie came in as he was talking and was told the whole tale. She, too, was left thoughtful by it.

"The simplest, most loyal thing to do," she said, "is to tell everything to the Commandant. Don't you think so? I'm sure he'd give up the idea of killing your fox."

"Maybe he would," said Piet, "but what about the others? They're very much against him. If the Commandant refuses to hunt him, they'll track him themselves. And sooner or later someone will catch him."

"Another thing," said Lina, "is that if we ask him, the Commandant will give up the idea of killing One-Toe. But it would be hard on him. And if the other hunters finally kill One-Toe anyway, he'd feel badly that we'd cheated him out of the fun of the hunt."

Tatie nodded. She agreed with Lina.

Piet described the places where he had met his friend and the way the fox had looked at him while slipping stealthily along through the bushes.

"He knows me, he really does. He looked at me, turning his head a little over his shoulder. I'm sure if I'd called him, he'd have stopped."

"Maybe he'd come to you," cried Gerard hopefully.

"If we were to feed him?" asked Genevieve.

No, Piet couldn't agree to that. One-Toe belonged in the forest. He should stay there.

"I know his lair," he said. "He's found himself a place that's well hidden and pleasant as can be. He'd miss it."

"How I'd like to see him!" cried Lina. "Do you think we might come with you?"

"W-e-l-l," said Piet.

"Just to see his lair! Please?"

Piet wasn't pleased at all by the idea. But he agreed it might be possible.

"And we could come too, couldn't we?" pleaded the twins.

"All right then, all right. I agree. But I warn you, it's a long way off. No complaints if you get too tired. Tatie, will you come too?"

"No," said Tatie, "I've too much work here. But I imagine you'll be able to take some great hikes before the real cold sets in."

"Tatie," said Lina, "please promise you won't tell the Commandant."

"I'm a neutral," said Tatie. "But don't forget, that fox wrecked my poultry yard."

Indian summer was exceptionally fine that year. Piet and his brother and sisters were able to visit the lair of One-Toe several times.

The first onset of cold had turned the leaves to the color of flame. Everywhere were sumptuous tones of deep red and gold. The undergrowth was already covered with dead leaves. The high bare treetops let the light penetrate in great oblique shafts. Blue mists slipped slowly between the high branches.

Sometimes the rapid flight of a herd of deer startled the young twin hikers and sent them back close to their elders. Piet enjoyed these walks much more than he'd first expected. He showed them the spots he'd discovered, pointing out their beauty. With a gesture like the Commandant's, he raised his arm to show them long perspectives that led their eyes toward infinity.

Lina and the children were delighted. They all came in at evening half dead with fatigue, muddy, but red-cheeked and with eyes still full of the enchantment of the things they'd seen.

"And One-Toe?" asked Tatie.

One-Toe stayed out of sight. Piet wasn't surprised. It would have been extraordinary if the fox had shown himself to strangers he could hear coming a mile off. As soon as he heard the noisy band, he probably hid under some bush and let the chattering crew go by.

That's what Piet thought, and he was quite right.

The first few times, One-Toe had been disturbed to find these small man-creatures coming up with such interest to his lair. He couldn't understand what they wanted near his house.

Several times, flattened in the underbrush, he watched their bright blue and red figures, heard their talk, and followed their progress. Among them was the one he already knew well and who had never tried to harm him.

Half reassured, he stayed on guard anyway. You never can tell. Caution comes first. So he stayed hidden. But his lively glance registered the image of the twins' blue jackets and Lina's red scarf and Piet's leaf-colored jacket.

However, one evening the children did see One-Toe.

It was at the end of a beautiful sun-filled afternoon. They'd made their usual visit to the lair that had become a sort of focus for their walks. Piet had shown them the fox's fresh tracks. They'd even picked up a smidgen of his fur that had rubbed off on the earth wall of his lair.

The children fell quiet, impressed by this isolated spot. The big pines that surrounded the clearing like a dark wall gave the place an air of mystery that overshadowed them with silence.

Across this silence the children heard the barking of a dog.

"Let's go," said Piet. "It's someone out hunting."

They left along the brook and plunged into the heart of the beech grove that covered one slope of the hill.

"Let's go see," said Piet. "Don't make any noise."

They climbed the height and from the summit looked down over a narrow valley that was covered with thick brush.

Once upon a time someone had tried to plant grape-vines on the sunny slopes. The little terraces with their rows of vines could still be made out. The attempt hadn't succeeded. The abandoned vines had developed with the wind's and sun's will, spreading out their branches among the briar that had soon invaded the site. Now it was all one tangled stretch of dense brush from which a few stunted trees rose.

It was from the midst of this undergrowth that the dog's barks came. The children were lying above it, in the grass, watching, not making a move.

"Oh," gasped Lina, "the Commandant!" She pointed upstream.

"There, against the oak tree."

They all saw him at the same moment. It was indeed the Commandant. They recognized his old felt hat, his hunting vest, his silhouette.

"Yes, it's he," whispered Piet.

The evening air was so limpid that every detail was sharp and clear. The children kept their eyes fixed on the face of their old friend. They'd never have thought that the Commandant's features could express such intense excitement. It wasn't anything like hate that showed in his face, but rather a kind of deep joy, which awed them.

He held his gun pointed toward the ground, but they felt that he was ready to fire if One-Toe should leave his hiding place.

He said nothing. He called no encouragement to his dog.

Taillefer came and went from one end to the other of the field, invisible in the underbrush. From time to time he barked in sharp little cries of "Nyap Nyap," or in a long full-throated call. He had to push slowly and painfully through tangled briar and grapevines. When a thorn tore his ears, he complained, muttering to himself. The children followed his desperate search intently. Sometimes they noticed, close to where they lay, a disturbance in the brush that might have been One-Toe.

The Commandant had noticed these disturbances too. They could see his attention was fixed on the bushes that covered the source of the suspicious sounds. They heard a sharp bird cry, a sort of song on four notes repeated several times. It happened twice before they understood that the Commandant used this means to call Taillefer, who came to his master at once.

The birdcall was so perfectly imitated that the children were staggered. One-Toe could easily be fooled by such a cry into coming within reach. That would be the end.

Once, they thought the end had come. The Commandant raised his gun to shoulder level.

"Oooh," gasped Lina.

The Commandant turned his head. The children ducked their noses into the grass.

What happened, exactly? Was One-Toe saved by Lina's cry? Had he noticed the hunter motionless under the tree? No one would ever know. But a few seconds later a russet flame darted from the undergrowth just opposite where the Commandant was standing.

"There he goes," whispered Piet.

The fox slipped along the bushes toward the woods on that side of the valley, while Taillefer looked for him at the opposite end of the brush.

What joy! The children beamed at each other. When they heard the bird cry again, they wanted to laugh aloud.

"Hush," said Piet. "Let's get out of here without standing up. Do what I do." He crawled backwards until he could stand without fear of being seen. The others followed. Then they stood and traipsed off toward the brook.

XII

One morning, as the house was in a turmoil of thorough cleaning, a loud horn blew in front of the mill. A splendid new station wagon stood there glittering.

A very tall, stout man with ruddy cheeks got out and stepped up to the door with authority. The twins, watching from behind their windows, saw he wore yellow boots and leather chaps like a cowboy.

The appearance of Tatie, her hair pulled back under a red scarf, more than ever like an Indian chief, made them hope for an extraordinary adventure.

But it went off quite quietly. The mechanized cowboy doffed his hat, presented himself, and a few seconds later they heard Tatie call.

"Quick, children, quick, they're waiting for you. Put on your jackets and boots. You're going hunting."

Piet and Lina were already dressed and talking to the newcomer in the living room.

Today was the great day. The evening before, the Commandant had sent a boy around to tell them that the next day they'd go after One-Toe. He had asked

Mr. de la Haute-Coindière to tell his friends and to bring the youngsters who'd been invited from the mill. There would be enough for everybody to do on this hunt.

Tatie gave them all a good hot drink of milk and coffee. Mr. de la Haute-Coindière had warned them that it was a sharp morning out of doors.

The car started with a fine spurt of speed. They were late; the hour for starting had been set for ten o'clock.

The day promised well. The forest shone. A trace of white frost was vanishing into the earth. On the holly branches, red bouquets of berries twinkled. Blue mists drifted slowly over the rosy briar patches.

Two cars were already parked outside the forest cabin from which the hunt would start.

The new arrivals were welcomed with cries of joy. The hunters Piet had met at the Commandant's house were there, along with three young red-checked farm boys. The ice was quickly broken. Mr. de la Haute-Coindière called everyone together and gave them instructions.

"The Commandant will be here soon," he said. "When he arrives, we'll start off."

"Why did he tell us not to bring dogs?" asked one.

"Taillefer will do the job better alone. I've had some cords prepared. Where did we put them?" he asked the boys.

"In the back of your station wagon."

"Cords?" asked Piet. "What does that mean?"

Lina cried, "Are you going to tie up the fox?"

The hunters laughed.

"Yes, Miss Lina, and you'll have the honor of making the knots."

They laughed all the more.

"Good," said Lina, who wasn't in the habit of backing down. "I'm an expert at knots; I promise he won't get free."

The young men were taking armsful of colored rags, feathers, and cords, all in a tangle, out of the trunk of the station wagon.

"Oh, I know," said Piet. "They're going to do a scarecrow hunt. I read about them in a book."

Lina and the twins looked at him. In the excitement of coming on a hunt and riding in this new station wagon, they'd forgotten that all these preparations were aimed at killing One-Toe.

"Now don't be silly," murmured Piet, "and don't say

a word. Do what we're asked. We'll be able to figure out what's best to do when we're on the spot."

They went closer and saw that the many-colored rags and the feathers—which were big tail feathers from geese and turkeys—were attached at intervals to fine strong cord. It made a great garland of bright colors that danced in the slightest breeze.

"I've had three hundred yards made," said Mr. de la Haute-Coindière. "I hope it'll be long enough."

Just then, glad voices greeted the arrival of the Commandant and Taillefer. The Old Gentleman was wearing his usual hunting costume.

He waved gaily at his young friends from the mill. Today he'd lost his habitual air of detachment.

When the children saw how much he took the hunt to heart, they felt a little guilty. Would they be able to act out their roles of traitor to the end? But then, they could not imagine letting poor One-Toe be slaughtered without trying to help him.

That night the fox had gone on a long hunt. He'd come back to his lair full and exhausted. He didn't wake until he heard his badger neighbors come in. Half

asleep, he listened to their murmurs in their adjoining rooms. He lay lazily in the good warmth of his fur until a rosy light came to the sill of his house. Subtle smells of roots and rotting acorns were wafted under his nose. Images of wild lavender bushes and orange rose-hips flitted through his head. And then he thought of the grapes.

The immense thicket that covered the wild grapevines was a place full of delights. Black grapes hung heavy from the bare vines. He had only to reach up and take them. Their sugary juice melted in his mouth. Whole multitudes of birds beat down in big flights onto the bushes. He'd more than once grabbed off a few stupefied sparrows or thrushes.

Rabbits came there in quantity too, to graze on the fresh grass. Surprising them was a game, as they hopped along their galleries that ran every which way.

One-Toe came out of his lair. The bright sun dazzled him. All was calm about his home. The still shadow of the pines was reassuring. Not a sound, only the singing brook waters tinkled through the silence. Great white clouds moved slowly across the blue sky.

The fox cleared his nose by sneezing two or three times, then began chasing fleas. This took several minutes. His fur was so thick that the parasites were crowded down underneath it. To scratch his spine, he had to roll on the ground and wiggle furiously.

From far off a jay cried out in its rusty voice, once. The bird was perhaps merely noting the passage of some rabbit. Off went the fox at a lively trot.

When he'd reached the top of the hill overlooking the wonderful slope covered with thickets, he recalled that the last time he'd been there a dog had troubled him. But he'd managed to get rid of the intruder.

The thickets were so dense and the passageways so intricate that it was unlikely he'd be taken by surprise in there.

In a few bounds, One-Toe was down the hill and had vanished under the bushes.

The abrupt flight of a band of sparrows he'd had his eye on surprised the fox. They were not flying from him. He was sure of that. Lying against a tuft of fern, his fur was well camouflaged by its browned leaves. And he hadn't stirred. Yet the birds had flown. It's true that the silly things fly off and alight for no reason at all. There'd be no point in looking to a sparrow for good sense. Yet a mild disquiet took root in One-Toe's mind.

Almost at once a brief bark told him that his tranquillity would be troubled again. He recognized the voice of the dog who just last week had stuck so to his tracks.

This dog was determined and harassing. There'd be no hope of tiring him out easily. The best defense would be to run off silently at once.

One-Toe listened carefully and, taking care not to stir the branches, slipped toward the other end of the field. Coming up behind the last curtain of brush, he stopped to listen. The dog wasn't even close. Perfect— he could leave the place without fear of being followed.

But an instinct for prudence held him back. Before him lay a wide bare space that he always avoided. Should he risk being caught there today?

For a minute he held himself prodigiously still, his every sense taut. And then he smelled tobacco.

Of course he didn't know that this sharp smell was made by tobacco. But each time he'd found it among the forest smells, the man was somewhere about. And he was danger itself. It would be fatal to run off to that side.

Softly he moved backward, slipping along belly to the ground, gliding between logs and tufts of roots. He came back to the center of the thicket. But soon he felt a general disquiet grow in the air about him. Rabbits were running, darting, in disorder, driven by the barking of the dog who was pursuing his chase in zigzags the whole width of the field.

The fact that he heard only one voice reassured One-Toe. He listened again. He heard twigs snap, far off to his left.

Without hesitation, he ran off to the right until he came to the edge of the thicket. The woods were close at hand. In two leaps he'd be safe.

He could already see the beeches' red leaves when he was stopped short by the movement of a strange thing.

It was white. It was blue. It was yellow. Here and there it was red. It floated a little above the ground. It moved. But it looked like nothing the fox had ever seen before. Neither plant nor animal, it was a frightening presence that strung out its length, clung to trees, dragged around bushes, tipped the grass in a silence charged with menace.

Shaking with fright, One-Toe backed off, his eyes fixed on the grimacing faces that the rags and feathers made across the shaded underbrush.

A bark from close by made him start. He broke away through the brush and ran to the other end of the field. The dog had heard him and was howling, full-voiced. He had to be quick. The welcoming shadow of the pine-wood was there. But he pulled up short once more. The same floating Thing was before his eyes, even more visible against the black of the pinewoods.

Shivering, he looked for another way out. But every-where loomed this barrier. He could not pass. It en-circled him and held him fast.

For several seconds he thought all was lost. But he regained the middle of the thicket and faced up to the precise known danger of the dog. He got back his control. The dog was far less frightening than the Thing around the thicket. With the dog he could use daring and cunning, and even force. He drove out his fear and turned resolutely to combat his enemy.

Taillefer nosed along, ardently examining all the bushes. One-Toe understood at once that he would never be able to hide in some nook under a root and wait this one out.

He'd have to move and keep moving, mixing his comings and goings so as to leave a tight trail of fresh scents that would be impossible for the dog to un-tangle.

So he began to run over the field, in every direction, mingling with the bewildered rabbits who didn't know whether to fear dog or fox more.

All this made for great confusion in the underbrush. It excited Taillefer, sent him on false tracks, and made the trackers and beaters call out, "Watch it! Here he comes! There he goes!"

Bursts of fire came from the guns. A few rabbits somersaulted. Then a sudden silence fell. Taillefer took up his quest again, and the furtive darting through the underbrush continued.

One-Toe began to think rather well of his situation. After all, the field was big enough and dense enough so that this game of hide and seek could go on till nightfall. He'd only have to watch out for the paths the dog took, avoid attracting his notice, stay clear of him, and, above all, not dash off blindly at any point. As he leaned, breathing hard, against a juniper bush, One-Toe heard something stir under a bush close by. Taillefer was far off. There could be no immediate danger.

But then he got a surprise. From out of the shadow of the bush came two dark forms headed for him. He recognized at once the couple of old gray foxes he'd met before.

More experienced than he, they'd stayed stock-still until now in their bush. They had known that the dog would follow the freshest track, so they had not moved at all, while One-Toe spread a network of tracks around.

And now what was it they wanted?

He soon found out. Without making a sound, the two animals jumped him and began pushing him with nips and bites toward the dog.

One-Toe understood their plan, then. They wanted to betray him to the hunters. Once he'd been strangled by the dog, the hunt would be over and the hunters would be satisfied. They'd leave the field, and the two cunning beasts would be able to go off in peace.

This was no time to fight them. He'd have to slip out of their clutches.

So off he ran, in a direction away from Taillefer. That wasn't what the brigands wanted. They separated to cut off his escape. But One-Toe was incredibly agile. Before the others could meet ahead of him, he'd run to the edge of the brush.

What a relief! The floating Things had vanished. One-Toe saw ahead of him a safe refuge in the woods. But he halted again, as he saw a group of hunters watching this end of the field. He couldn't cross in front of them. And his trackers were coming in close. But from behind the curtain of undergrowth they, too, had seen the hunters. At shouts from the men, the two brigands fled.

This time it was One-Toe who stayed stock still. He carefully watched the group that was talking excitedly a few feet away from him.

The flight of the two brigands hadn't gone unnoticed. "There are two of them, two of them!" cried the three village youngsters to the hunters.

Piet and the others said not a word. They had seen

the two animals, but they knew they hadn't seen One-Toe's red fur.

Their companions, highly pleased with themselves, went off to tell Mr. de la Haute-Coindière what they'd seen—two foxes instead of one, and beauties too.

"I'm sure they didn't see One-Toe," said Piet.

"Maybe he's not there at all," said Lina. "Maybe the Commandant made a mistake."

"Maybe, but I don't think the Commandant makes mistakes often."

While the children held counsel, One-Toe, who was only a few yards from them, didn't budge.

On his left he saw the Things that stretched on the two long sides of the field. But straight ahead, where the children were, was a clear space.

The reason was simple. The fright-cord Mr. de la Haute-Coindière had made wasn't long enough to encircle the thicket completely. It had seemed best to protect only the two long sides of the field with the fright-cords. The children could keep watch at one end, and the hunters would take the other.

The children talked in low tones. One-Toe stared at them with foxy anxiety. In his mind a familiar image rose up. He recognized the blue outlines of the little ones, Lina's scarf and Piet's jacket. He'd often passed by close to them.

"Don't move," said Piet. "He's right there. He's to the right behind that tuft of furze. He's looking at us. Don't turn around."

A gunshot rang out. There were shouts of "Get him,

get him!" Another shot, and a third and a fourth, were followed by shouts of triumph.

One-Toe slipped along beside the bushes. The children stayed still and quiet as statues.

"He's going," said Piet. "He's saved."

One-Toe had reached the cover of the trees. His supple outline could scarcely be seen as it glided over the leaf-covered earth.

The village boys came galloping up. "Come on! They've got them!"

"Let's run," said Piet.

The two gray old-timers lay stretched side by side in the grass. Taillefer watched them suspiciously, as if he expected them to jump up and away again. The hunters were exultant. They all talked at once, telling how they'd seen first one and then another fox come tearing along.

"We saw them first," cried the lads from the village.

Everyone agreed that Taillefer was a fantastic dog. At the end, he'd driven the two beasts so hard and close that the hunters were almost afraid they would shoot him as well.

"Yes, it's wonderful," said Mr. de la Haute-Coindière. "Wonderful. But where's One-Toe?"

Everyone turned to look at the Commandant, who stood thoughtfully filling his pipe.

"It looks as though you were mistaken, for once, old friend."

And, naturally, no one was very sorry to see the invincible Commandant caught in a mistake.

"The fact is that One-Toe wasn't there. And yet you were sure he was, weren't you?"

"Yes," the Commandant admitted. "I was sure. And I don't understand it at all."

The others burst out laughing jovially. After all, they'd taken a fine quarry and it made them all feel extra good to see that the best-known hunter in the whole region could make mistakes like anyone else. The glory of the day went to One-Toe who'd fooled everyone else there and now had fooled the Commandant too.

The children exchanged glances. Piet made a signal to be quiet.

But Lina shrugged. "I beg your pardon," she said distinctly. "You're all wrong, and the Commandant didn't make a mistake. One-Toe *was* there."

"Ho! That's a good one," someone roared, and everyone laughed again. Lina's voice had been so full of fight that it sounded as if she'd tell any lie to defend the honor of her friend the Commandant.

"One-Toe was there."

"And did you see him, Miss? I suppose you saw his little white tail hop along cute as could be!"

"You saw a rabbit," cried the village boys. "It was a rabbit you saw."

"They think I'm a fool," thought Lina, wrinkling her forehead.

The Commandant was watching her without a word. He gave her a wink and a little nod of approval.

"After all," she said, "maybe it was a rabbit."

XIII

"You know, sir, it really was One-Toe. Lina wasn't just inventing it to make you feel good. He went past right by us. I recognized him."

They were standing at the edge of an oak wood that sheltered them from the stiff winds.

It was a sunny, cold afternoon of a day when the northwest wind blew strong. After several days of spitting rain brought by warm ocean winds, frost had come, hard and sudden, seizing the earth, freezing the grass, stripping the trees of their brilliant autumn color.

The woods had taken on their winter aspect. You could see great distances above the young undergrowth of the chestnut trees, against the tall beechwood and the borders of hazelnut trees. Clouds soared long and far, suspended in the blue, above the deserted dales.

The Commandant stuffed his pipe slowly and carefully tamped it down. He smiled.

"I know," he said. "I know."

Piet was tempted to tell all. Something held him back. Perhaps the air of satisfaction in face and attitude of his companion stopped him. The Commandant seemed

happy to have failed. One-Toe still ran free, and so much the better.

"Were you sure he was in the thicket?"

"Yes. I'd followed him for several days, and I knew that on sunny afternoons he went to that old abandoned vine. Animals have their habits, just as people do."

"And of course you expected to get him?"

"Frankly, yes. But"—he began to laugh—"it would have been a pity."

"A pity?"

"Yes, a pity for him, a pity for me, and a pity for the art of hunting. I'd have regretted it if we had taken him."

Now it was Piet's turn to laugh. "May I tell you a story, sir?" he said. And he began to recite. "Hear the famous fable of the fox and the sour grapes."

"Right," said the Commandant. "You've no idea how right you are. Here's how I feel about One-Toe. It's a little as if someone gave you a bunch of magnificent grapes that hadn't quite ripened. You might taste them and even eat them. But don't you think you'd always regret you hadn't waited a few days longer before picking them? They'd have been infinitely better. Your pleasure in them would have been tripled. That's how I feel about One-Toe."

"Do you mean, sir, that One-Toe isn't ripe and ready yet?"

"That's about it. He's already a real competitor, and he has a lot of tricks to his bag. But he'll learn a good many more if he has the chance. And imagine what a magnificent opponent he'll be then."

"Then you still hope to get him some day?"

"Certainly, what do you suppose? I'll beat him, but by the rules. What happened the other morning gives me every hope of his being a really great master of cunning. If my Taillefer had been able to force him out of that thicket despite the fact that it's perfect cover . . . or if he'd come out where we could shoot him despite the hunters with guns who kept talking and smoking . . . or if he hadn't been able to tell hunters from beaters . . . then frankly I'd have been disappointed, do you see? One-Toe would have disappointed me. He'd not have been what I hoped, the gallant fox his earlier deeds had made me hope he was. That's the story."

Piet listened without answering. He tried to hide his sorrow. He'd hoped that One-Toe would be able to live in peace in the woods from now on. He'd been completely mistaken. Not only would the fox be in constant danger, but he'd be hunted with more and more subtle traps. Every time he'd win his escape, he'd be a bigger prize for the hunters. And finally, one day, he'd be taken.

What would the twins and Lina say when they learned that the hunt of the other day was only the first of many hard tests their friend would undergo? Piet was sure the hunters would finally win out.

How could he tell them such news? How explain

that the Commandant whom they all loved, who was so good, and who was their friend, was determined to go on until he'd killed One-Toe. It would be awful if the others were to decide in favor of the fox and begin to hate the old man.

"You seem to be dreaming, my boy. What are you thinking of?"

"I thought that you loved the forest and the animals," said Piet.

The Commandant watched him a moment, then turned aside.

"Excepting children," he said, "there's nothing in the world I love half so much as the forest and the animals."

It was already coming to the turning of the year. Days were lengthening. The young chestnuts had a lovely purple color, and flowery cattails hung trembling from hazel and alder trees.

The wind blew cold, then warm, then warm and rain-laden. Now and then a snow cloud passed over and left the forest white and silent.

One golden morning the hunters ran across One-Toe's tracks again. The Commandant looked carefully at the print of his mutilated foot.

"It's his, right enough. He's just passed this way, within the last few minutes. Let's follow him," he said.

He bade Taillefer to heel and be quiet.

They walked in silence. The tracks went in wide curves that Piet couldn't understand.

Soon another track appeared.

"Ah, there we are," said the Commandant, as if he'd expected this.

Piet recognized the print of a deer. One-Toe must have followed it, circling downwind, for a long time. Probably it had been a hurt or sick animal that its herd had abandoned.

"It's the law of the forest," said the Commandant. "The individual must be sacrificed, if he endangers the welfare of the tribe."

"And One-Toe takes advantage of lone animals like this one?"

"Yes. He realizes that one lone deer is an easy prey. He's right—the creature was done for anyway."

They went no farther that day. But some days later they found more fox tracks near the thicket of wild vines where the great hunt had taken place.

Again Taillefer was told to be silent and still at the foot of the tree where the Commandant stood. Piet went a little farther on, behind a big oak.

They'd come up under the wind, and their steps were muffled by a ground cover of soft snow.

"How does the Commandant know that One-Toe will come along this side? He might just as well decide to slip out along the other side of the field. It's all a matter of luck," Piet thought.

But it wasn't all a matter of luck.

Piet had been behind this tree for a few minutes when he heard a series of little rabbit cries.

One minute, two—nothing happened.

The cries began again. The creature must be there, close, about to leap into view. Of course, it wouldn't be what the Commandant wanted. It was the fox he was after, not a wretched little rabbit.

There was the noise again.

Piet turned around and began to laugh. There wasn't any rabbit. It was the Commandant who was making those perfect rabbit noises. He stood a little bent, his gun over his arm, his eyes intent on the edge of the thicket.

A slight shaking in the brush could just be heard. Piet at once lost all desire to laugh. One-Toe had been drawn by the cries and was very close. If he crossed the edge of the thicket, he'd be lost.

There was a dreadful silence. The Commandant now had his gun in both hands. Again the little stirring among the leaves could be heard.

Then came a snapping of twigs and the sound of a rapid flight.

The Commandant put his gun over his shoulder.

"It's no good," he said. "He wins this round. Perhaps next time we'll fool him."

XIV

One-Toe was turning into a legend without knowing it. He lived his fox life, cunning and daring. The vast forest he crisscrossed with his silent rapid trot was a friend whose expressions he knew well: the high treetops lifting their rustling branches against the sky, the bare underwoods, the heath-covered clearings, the rocky ravines, the shallow valleys, and the sunny slopes prickly with furze and eglantine.

He knew which were dangerous passages and which were sure ways out. Every noise that his acute ears heard had its meaning, and even silence spoke to him. The repeated cry of a jay told him from a distance of the presence of some animal. Depending on time and place, he'd come closer or run off, always as ready to attack as to flee. Everything served him—the bark of a farm dog out marauding on his own, the yapping of another fox, the path the deer took, the call of a night bird, the swoop of a hawk.

His nostrils registered the scents of animals and plants, and the earth smells as well. He drew some information from each of the thousand warnings that came to him from sight, sound, and scent.

He wasn't some miraculous beast, as the farmers thought. But he had, in a few short months, acquired a lot of experience. Every day gave him more opportunities to increase his prudence and shrewdness.

Toward mid-February, winter cold still gripped the earth and frosted the branches. The wind whistled; the ribbons of snow circled the foot of the hedges. But where there was protection from the cold wind, the sun was already high enough to warm the edges of the furze. Sap began to surge up into the high branches. Under the old dried grass new grass began to spring green. The last dead leaves, those of the oaks, rustled and shook in a mass.

And one day the big west winds brought warm rain, a gentle steady rain that covered the hills with greenish mud, melted the snow, and filled the valleys with the song of brooklets.

Life took on a new lease. The woods rang with calls and cries and wild races.

Big stags engaged in furious combat deep in lonely thickets. The clash of their antlers resounded in the ravines. New families were started and soon began to build nests or arrange lairs.

One-Toe, too, felt himself carried away by the vast stirring within the forest.

One evening, near the brook, he saw a furious little creature being chased by two wicked-looking old gray foxes. It was a young delicate vixen who, seeing her retreat cut off by One-Toe, gave a sharp cry of distress. But it wasn't the inoffensive vixen One-Toe was after. He was indignant with the two males who were coming up on either side of the brook, snarling and whining at each other. They had dared to intrude on his domain.

When they saw One-Toe's black outline against a high slope of rock, they stopped, their jowls drawn back, their fur standing up.

His rights had been invaded, and One-Toe was enraged. He took advantage of his place above the intruders and leaped down on one of them. His weight hit the miscreant hard and tumbled him pellmell into the underbrush. Caught out in a territory he didn't know well, not sure of what the other old fox would do, he decided to run off. One-Toe dashed after him, and they tumbled in a wild course down toward the bottom of the ravine.

One-Toe had nothing against continuing the chase, but the intruder ran fast and he saw no reason to go too far afield. Besides, he was always a trifle hampered in racing by his injured paw. He barked a few warnings after the coward. Then he had a long drink from the brook and went back up the slope to his domain.

He was scarcely halfway up when the noise of a fight made him hurry. It sounded close to his lair.

Troubled, One-Toe listened and sniffed as he went. The night was full of smells and cries of all kinds. Calls and defiant howls mingled with the songs of night birds.

At the clearing, One-Toe saw shadowy forms near his

lair. He at once recognized his two white-headed neighbors who were yapping at a third shape with pointed
ears.

One-Toe gave his war cry. The second gray fox at
once leaped aside and fled without asking any further
questions.

The two badgers turned with one movement and
stalked back into their house.

Dawn was near. Hungry with all the excitement,
One-Toe went toward the rabbit warrens. As usual the
stupid creatures were leaping and dancing in the early
dawn light. He had only to seize what he wanted.

The sun was rising on the plain when he got back
home. Before slipping into his lair, he shook off the
dew that clung to his fur, rolled in the sand, and
scratched himself against a log. At daylight, he finally
decided to enter his house.

He had just stuck his nose in when he yanked it out
again, with a cry of pain. Two long scratches stood red
on his nose.

Indignant and surprised, One-Toe made a grimace,
turned in a circle, and finally headed back for his hole.

The intruder was there, ready to scratch and bite.
Suddenly One-Toe understood. He had recognized the
little vixen. When the second old fox had tried to over-
take her, she'd found refuge in the first hole she saw,
while her tormentor found himself up against the two
badgers.

One-Toe, reassured, made a few friendly noises. The
vixen pretended to hear nothing. He continued his

peaceful proposals. When she didn't reply, he went to stretch out in a fern patch, keeping his eyes on the entrance to his hole.

And that is how luck brought One-Toe a companion.

She was gentle and peaceful and became quickly attached to One-Toe. She never got over the impression that she had won their lair in a noble battle. Soon she knew their kingdom as well as One-Toe did and was as vigilant as he in keeping their frontiers safe.

In the full glory of spring their cubs were born. April sun flooded the underwoods. The forest hummed with insects hovering over the flowering trees. The cuckoos' song was caught up in the echoes and sounded through the valleys.

One-Toe stared curiously at his sons. There were three of them, three little balls of plush snuggled close to their mother. Full of milk, they slept and woke only to drink again greedily.

The first few days they only stirred a little and made small, plaintive sounds. They began to blink one eye, then the other, showing two tiny gray spots with a bluish light.

The vixen was devoted to her babies and never left them. One-Toe didn't think they looked much like foxes yet, with their round heads and their ears that were hardly pointed at all. Nevertheless, he regarded them with a feeling of tenderness and would have liked to be of some use to them. But his spouse wanted him only to bring her food.

With devoted fury he attacked the creatures in the

nearby woods. Then, thinking he'd best leave the closer prey for his wife who would soon want to feed herself and the babies as she pleased, he went farther off. He went down into the plain and began to devastate the henhouses and rabbit hutches of the farmers.

Once again, One-Toe's tracks were seen everywhere. The farmers' wives ranted against him because he was devouring their broods of baby chicks. They nagged their husbands to catch the thief. But the farmers were too busy with spring planting to be able to go running off after a fox. They said their wives should watch the poultry yards more carefully.

So One-Toe and his family lived in a plentiful peace. Food was abundant and good. The little ones grew while he looked at them. In a few weeks they were playing on the threshold of the lair. Their mother let them wrestle with the bones of One-Toe's prey. They played and had mock fights with their paws.

The clearing was quiet. No intruder dared approach the domain that was now guarded by two young, strong animals. The vixen had lost her mild airs since her babies were born. She was a first-rate defender of their home now.

But once she almost lost one of her babies.

It was late on a May afternoon. She had been hunting part of the night while her spouse had watched the house. Now she was drowsing near the lair while the little ones played in the warm sand. They were lively and full of tricks. She lay dreaming with half-shut eyes, happy and peaceful.

In the clearing, all was still. A family of tomtits sprang about in the pine branches, stuffing themselves with yellow caterpillars.

Suddenly the vixen opened her eyes. A sharp silence had alerted her. The birds had flown off.

She turned her head to every side. All seemed calm. The little ones rolled in the sand. Yet she wasn't reassured. She raised her eyes and sprang up with a cry.

A gray shadow dropped from the sky like a piece of lead. A hawk! The little ones knew from her cry that danger was near and instinctively went onto their backs, their claws standing out from their tiny paws.

The pirate saw her flame-colored shadow spring from the bushes, just as he swooped close to one of the little ones. She smashed into him hard. Then she pushed her babies beneath her, as the hurt bird beat his wings wildly and took off into the pinewood.

It had been a sharp warning, and from then on the vixen watched even more closely over her family.

The day the west wind had brought the first spring rains, Piet and the Commandant had been walking near the village of Mervent, quite far from the chateau. They'd stopped in a blacksmith shop to dry out their soaked clothes. Because of the bad weather, a good many farmers had brought in their tools to be repaired. The forge was full of men who, forced to stop work for the day, were in no hurry to leave. They began telling stories of the countryside. Naturally One-Toe was soon the topic of conversation. The Commandant, de-

lighted to find such interested listeners, told many tales with great success.

The quick-witted farmers had their own tales to tell, too. For every one of the Commandant's tall tales, some farmer had one to top it. It wasn't long before the talk ascended into the realm of the fantastic—a true hunters' paradise.

The blacksmith, who had heard such encounters at his forge before, smiled into his mustache and tapped away vigorously. The fire blazed. Sparks leaped out onto the ground and the steamy clothes. It was cozy and cheerful. The sound of hearty laughter roared above the patter of rain on the round roof tiles.

"I got my death of cold in there," said the Commandant, a few days later.

"Too cold, then too hot. That's not very prudent," scolded Tatie, who had hurried over as soon as she'd heard the Commandant was abed. "You should be more careful. What does the doctor say?"

"The doctor is in the doctor business—he says I'm sick."

"You must listen to him, and do every single thing he says."

The doctor had stated plainly that the Commandant had been very sick indeed and would need a long time to complete his convalescence.

"If you can get him to be patient with his own recovery, he'll be fine after a while," he advised Tatie.

"Bring me visitors," cried the Commandant between coughs. "I've got a lot of stories to tell."

The twins were stricken by the looks of their sick friend. They couldn't help being surprised at how thin and weak he'd become. And the Commandant saw their surprise.

"I'm a selfish old man," he told Tatie. "Don't bring them again until I've stopped looking like something the cat dragged in."

But Piet came anyway. Every day after school he went round the long way home to see his friend.

The doctor was right; it took a long time for the Commandant to regain his strength. But he was a good patient. He took his medicine and obeyed orders and was careful. Tatie was delighted; Piet was, too, but he was even more surprised. It seemed to him that the Commandant was hiding a plan or getting ready to play a good joke on someone.

Fair weather had been with them for some time. Afternoons, the Commandant took a slow stroll round the pond, Taillefer with him. They talked, dog and master, and kept each other company in a conversation full of thoughtfulness and meditation. Piet would find them, come evening, in the library where a good blaze burned in the hearth. There, the old man showed the boy his inner thoughts. It was no series of lectures, but quiet conversation that gave Piet a chance to piece together his friend's ways of thinking.

Their talk centered around the woods and its creatures. The Commandant let his memories flow, told of some remarkable hunts, brought back to momentary life the animal heroes he'd finally conquered.

Chief among his memories were the stories of a certain few foxes whom he'd conquered in honorable combat. They were for him like old friends whose glories and courage he was happy to recall and praise.

"But not one of them was the equal of One-Toe!" was the way the best of these tales ended, every time.

Piet learned that the thought of One-Toe seldom left the back of the old man's mind. In fact, the memories he recalled were just as much in praise of One-Toe, the one fox he hadn't been able to down.

"Heaven and St. Hubert, Patron of Hunters, have been kind to me. I hope I deserve it."

Piet said nothing; he was afraid he understood.

"The most handsome, the most intelligent. Oh, a splendid beast! Remember the day he escaped the fright-cords? And the other time, when he used the two old foxes to throw us off the scent? I read and reread every track. No author has ever had the pleasure of writing about such a magnificent specimen."

His eyes bright, his cheeks rosy, he pulled out book after book where the hunting wisdom of twenty generations was stored. Then he gestured toward the forest just beyond the walls. "You see," he said, "I haven't been quite fair with him. He's no animal to hunt down with ordinary methods. The fright-cords and the decoy-rabbit-whistling were too crude for him to be fooled by. He's a creature of noble qualities that demand our respect."

"Yes," said Piet, fast. "We should have left him in peace."

"In peace? Never! He's a fighter. All he needs are foes worthy of his abilities, hunters who understand and appreciate what a remarkable fellow he is."

He thought a few minutes. "A day is coming when I'll go out again. I'll get to know his lair and his habits. He'll find me wherever he goes. I won't stoop to tricks or treachery. He'll know that I'm a foe worthy of him. We'll fight it out honorably, one against the other."

He smiled dreamily. "He'll be my last fox," he said. "When he and I have done, I'll hang up my gun."

When Piet told the others this, back at the mill, they were dismayed. Several times the twins went to the lair hoping to find it empty. If only One-Toe were to disappear from the region, were to go to some other forest, how much better they'd feel!

"But he's just as likely to be killed somewhere else," reasoned Tatie.

"Yes, but we wouldn't have to know about it," said Lina.

"When you think of it," said Piet, "we're like the Commandant. We can't seem to get One-Toe out of our minds."

Spring was everywhere in its full splendor. The forest was an enchanted palace of pleasures. The children found whole valleys carpeted in jonquils, and under-woods dense with periwinkles. There were softly mys-terious clearings illuminated by long slants of sun. There were sudden showers followed by rainbows that garlanded the forest.

They'd begun their evening walks once more. The flatland sang with a thousand crickets. Along the brook, the frogs piped.

Mascot came and went. Despite their high hopes, he was still no hunter. He shook with fear at every strange noise in the hedges along their way.

Almost a whole year had gone by, and it seemed that nothing had changed. Tatie's poultry was coming along well, and even making money. The children's father had begun to work again, though their mother still had to help out. It had been decided that the children should stay with Tatie until the end of the school year. But when vacations were over, they'd return to Paris.

Of course, they'd be back to visit. Tatie said loudly

that she'd be glad to see the last of them. That was her way of making their going easier. She used it to hide her feelings and cover up how much she'd miss them.

All was well, then, save for the unsettled war between the Commandant and One-Toe. Piet told them the news each day, and it wasn't cheering. The Commandant was living in expectation of the time when he'd be out in the woods again. He was watching out for his health and following the doctor's orders to make that day come more quickly.

"I won't be able to help One-Toe this time," said Piet. "I know the Commandant wants to be alone. He won't take me along with him. He wants to settle the contest singlehanded."

One Thursday afternoon the twins were bringing grain for the chickens up to the poultry yard. They heard barking in the forest, near its edge.

"It's Taillefer," said Gerard.

They set down their sacks against the fence and scampered home.

Piet was already out on the embankment, listening.

"It's Taillefer," cried the twins.

"You're right," Piet agreed, with a frown.

Lina ran out of the kitchen, her arms covered with flour. "Isn't that Taillefer?" she cried.

The barks resounded again, higher up the hill.

"It is, it's he, I knew it. We've got to go out there right away."

Lina unknotted her apron, calling, "Tatie, Tatie."

Tatie came to the door. "I heard it too," she said worriedly. "Where are you going? Just what do you plan to do?"

Her face was as anxious as the children's. She looked from one pair of troubled eyes to the other.

"Tatie," said Lina, "Piet says One-Toe has babies in the lair. If the Commandant kills him, they'll die of hunger."

"True," said Piet.

"I don't want the fox cubs to die," said Genevieve, almost sobbing.

"Don't cry," scolded Tatie. "That's all we need." She waved her long arms. "You don't want, you don't want —it's easy to say, but what can I do? I'm no magician, after all."

"Tatie, if you were to explain to the Commandant, he'd understand."

"Explain? What? That he musn't kill foxes? But I loathe foxes myself. They slaughtered my chickens. The Commandant knows that as well as you do. If I were to ask him to leave the foxes alone, he'd think me mad, and he'd be right."

"Not all foxes, Tatie. Just our fox, just One-Toe."

"Your fox? You call him yours because your silliness hurt his foot in the trap. I didn't put those traps out. You children! It'll be a lovely, quiet, calm, peaceful day when you all go back to Paris."

But as she stormed away, Tatie was taking off her apron and putting on her walking shoes.

Lina winked at Piet and shooed the twins quietly off to get their boots on.

They were just ready when Tatie said, "Well, what are you waiting for? Come on, but first lock up Mascot."

"Oh, poor Mascot," the twins cried.

"All right then, bring him along. We might as well make a complete mess while we're about it."

The family trooped out, and Tatie shut the door with its big old double lock.

She lined the children up and said, shaking her finger sternly, "Now listen. Between your fox and the Commandant, it's the Commandant I choose. You must understand that much. It wouldn't be right to spoil his dearest pleasure. Piet's told you plainly enough how much he wants to catch the fox. You prefer to consider the animal. That's your affair. I'll limit myself to telling the Commandant simply what idiots you are. That's all."

That afternoon, One-Toe had left his lair early. His cubs were now so hungry that he had to hunt day and night. The vixen had only brought back a young rabbit at dawn. It wasn't enough for a whole day.

One-Toe had decided to go off in the direction of the farms. The spring chickens were now big enough to be interesting, and still young and stupid enough to wander from their yards toward the woods.

As he ran across a field of brake, One-Toe heard a pheasant cock give a cry of alarm. It was off to his right, near a beechwood.

He stopped to listen. Camouflaged by the sharp-toothed leaves, he felt in no danger. But he had to know what had upset the pheasant.

He didn't stir for several minutes. The leaves hid him, but also prevented him from having a good look around. He had best not linger in that place.

He was about to go on his prudent way when he noticed a light sound behind him.

At once he slipped off toward the trees. Though he was as careful as possible, his passage was marked by a sort of wake where the ferns bent before him, so before he left cover, he looked right and left. It was a good thing he did. At the far end of the field was a silent gray figure. One-Toe recognized it at once. It was one of those quiet hunters who watch for you along the most secret paths, the worst, deadliest kind of man.

Gliding along under cover, close to the woods' edge, the fox took himself off fast. There was no point in precautions now; he'd been seen.

When he came to the angle of the field, he leaped into the woods and sped away.

A whistle warned him he'd been seen again. Barking broke out at once. A dog was on his fresh tracks. It would be a hard contest. He hadn't known it, but he must have been followed for some time—perhaps even since he'd left the lair.

At the thought of his home, he was filled with dread. He'd have to be careful to stay well away from there.

For several minutes he ran straight ahead, intent on putting all the space he could between himself and his trackers. But he was up against a dangerous foe. Its voice echoed in his every nerve. He recognized that bark, as he did the bark of every dog that frequented the woods. Though he had never found the loud yaps of the farm dogs frightening, Taillefer's bark meant the worst kind of trouble.

Little by little his first fears diminished. He knew the country they ran over thoroughly. He called to mind the different spots of thick cover he might use for shelter, the passageways he ordinarily used, and the location of old animal diggings where he might stop to catch his breath.

He went off to the right, then to the left, trying to dislodge the dog if only for a few minutes. But he soon saw that this trick, which might do for sheep dogs, didn't disturb Taillefer at all. This dog wouldn't give up or be fooled. It would take patience to lead him from cover to cover as far from the High Place as possible.

So One-Toe began a spiraling movement at some distance from the woods' edge. If he had to, he'd circle around the whole of Mervent Forest until night sheltered him.

He pulled himself together for a long run. That made him feel more tranquil. He could count on his tough muscles and strong wind not to betray him. He'd last until nightfall.

But he soon saw that things wouldn't work out that way. He'd headed down a path toward Long Brook when a flash came from under the trees. A burning wind zipped along his flank and a thousand thorny points stung his skin.

The barking, coming from all sides, still stormed about his ears.

Echoes multiplied Taillefer's cries and filled the valley with the sound of menace.

One-Toe ran up the stiff slope, followed by howls that drove him unwillingly toward the center of the forest.

As soon as the vixen heard the far-off sounds of barking, she gathered her little ones together and herded them inside. Then she flattened herself within the entrance to the hole. Ears and nose sharply attentive, she turned herself into a solid unit of watchful mistrust.

The blunt echo of the rifle shot made her shiver. She listened until the barking began once more, reassuring her that the hunt wasn't over. The shot hadn't hit its mark. But what was being hunted? As the minutes went by, she grew more anxious.

One-Toe must know what was going on. And if, knowing, he didn't come to her, it was because he himself was the object of the hunt. She could count on him to lead the hunter away from their home. He was a father and would, like any parent, protect his young.

Her heart beat hard as she followed the sounds of the chase. What could be happening? Had One-Toe thrown the dog off his trail? Had he found a safe refuge in some solid lair where he could stand off his enemies?

Suddenly the barks broke out close by, on the other slope behind the pinewood. The vixen shuddered. It couldn't be One-Toe. He couldn't have come this way for safety. It must be some careless young fox who was making instinctively for the deepest part of the forest to hide himself.

A new danger rose in her mind. What if the hunted animal were to come by and think the lair empty? He'd be sure to run into it to hide. That could be a catastrophe for her family. She'd have to take precautions.

She went back to her babies and pushed them into the deepest part of the house, warning them to stay there no matter what happened.

The shot made the children stop stock-still. It came from their left, in the depths of the little valley. The twins were ready to cry as they all stood silent.

A few minutes later they heard more barking.

"He missed," said Piet.

He ran toward the height, but the dense trees kept him from seeing anything. One thing was certain. The hunt was still on.

"Where's the Commandant?" murmured Lina.

"He must be watching the passages along the other slope."

"Suppose we call him?"

"No. The fox must be near here. If we call out, he'll think we're hunting him too. We might send him smack into range of the Commandant's rifle. Be quiet as we can."

Then the twins cried, "There he is!",

They pointed to the next hill. It was covered with a few bare rocks, between which rose up the gnarled roots of oak trees. Piet and Lina saw a rusty flash dash across and into the trees.

"He's saved," cried Lina.

But at once Taillefer's voice rang out, and his dark silhouette sped among the rocks. In a wink the basset had vanished after the fox.

Just then, Tatie cried out, "Mascot, Mascot!"

Mascot had slipped his leash and was running off in the underbrush.

After a few minutes, his yapping sounded from the right.

"He's completely off the track," said Piet. "He won't do One-Toe any harm. Poor Commandant. He'll be furious. And Taillefer! I wouldn't blame him if he strangled Mascot for this."

The children exulted, but Tatie frowned. "What an idiot I was to come out with you," she said. "Now what? Piet, for heaven's sake lead us to the Commandant, so I can explain. Where do you think he is?"

"I expect he's waiting for One-Toe over in the other ravine."

"Good, let's go find him there. Come along." Tatie went down the slope with long strides, followed by the children.

The Commandant wasn't at the bottom of the ravine. Nor was he on the next hill, nor in the other ravine.

Piet didn't understand. He'd have sworn that the

Commandant would be along the trails he knew well. Perhaps he'd given up the hunt because Mascot had come galumphing in to spoil it. The barking they'd been hearing off and on had stopped now.

Piet led the others, not sure what to do, toward the High Place. When they came out at the bottom of the valley, Taillefer's bark broke out in the pinewood. Mascot's sharp bark answered from the right.

A form appeared at the edge of the wood. It was the Commandant. He turned and saw the children. His face was full of joy.

"Marvelous, marvelous," he called to them. "He's wonderful. Taillefer isn't pleased of course, but . . ."

"But what?" asked Lina, amazed.

"But Mascot—he's done a splendid job. It's perhaps not in the usual rules of the hunt. But I never saw anything like it. Whether he knew it or not, he dashed in and cut off One-Toe's line of escape. He drove the fox for me, as well as if he'd been a pack of hounds. You've come at just the right moment. One-Toe's right over there, in that little thicket. Watch out. He'll be coming out soon. Taillefer's forcing him on."

They were all silent.

Noises came from the thicket.

"Tatie," Lina whispered to her aunt. "Isn't it time to tell him now?"

"Yap!" said Taillefer.

A russet streak shot past and vanished again in the brambles. The Commandant had shouldered his gun.

He let it fall and turned stammering to Piet. "But . . .
but . . . it's not One-Toe at all. Did you see? It's
not One-Toe, it's a little vixen."

Suddenly Taillefer's fanfare broke out in triumph
and went off in the direction of the pines.

"There he goes, One-Toe himself. He's tricked me.
And the little vixen has got off safe, too."

He whistled with two fingers to his lips. Then he
said, "What I can't quite understand is at which point the
vixen mixed her tracks with his. With the racket those
dogs were making, normally any fox for miles around
would have taken to his lair. But this one seems to have
come out of her lair on purpose, just to confuse me.
Amazing."

Taillefer, who was sniffing right and left, displeased at
having been called back, shot out suddenly, furiously.
Mascot followed on his heels, and the the two dogs
vanished in the direction of the High Place.

"Let's go see what's happening," said the Commandant.

They came up to the little sunny clearing, green and
gold between its tall pine walls.

Mascot was barking like a madman and sniffling
around the entrance to One-Toe's lair. Now and then
he scratched the earth furiously, making the dirt fly ten
feet behind him.

They stopped a little way off. The Commandant
said, "I don't understand. The lair must be empty. I
last saw One-Toe at least half a mile away from here. He
did everything he could to lead me away until Mascot

cut him off and made him come back up this way. And yet the dogs have found a fresh scent, right here."

"Didn't you say there was a vixen?" asked Piet.

"Yes—she must have come out at the last minute, just to save One-Toe!"

The children listened without saying a word. Mascot kept on digging.

"Anyway, she did what she intended to," murmured Lina.

"Who?"

"The vixen saved her babies' father. One-Toe got away from you!"

"Right," said the Commandant. "He got away again." He added, smiling, "You almost sound glad of it."

"Oh, but I am," cried Lina.

At that point Mascot's barks shot up into higher key.

He was leaping into the air, all four feet off the ground, coming down on all fours, and leaping again.

Taillefer's rear end appeared at the entrance to the lair. He was pulling something toward him that didn't seem easy to lift. Mascot barked his head off. Taillefer made a noise in his throat. He turned so they could see, caught lightly in his mouth, a small brown ball that he brought in triumph to the Commandant's feet.

The children had exclaimed in horror at first, but changed quickly to cries of delight. "Isn't he cute? Isn't he marvelous? See that! He looks just like a tiny bear."

Belly to the ground, the fox cub rolled frightened eyes.

Taillefer nosed at the little creature. It waved a needle-sharp set of claws, and the dog backed off, pretending he was afraid.

Mascot circled around the plushy ball, wagging his tail.

Taillefer dashed back into the lair.

A minute later he emerged with a second small prisoner, who dove in close to his brother.

The children danced for joy.

When Taillefer came out again with a third fox cub, the twins clapped their hands. Tatie laughed. "Well anyway, the race of foxes isn't extinct yet."

"Absurd, the absolute height of absurdity," moaned the Commandant. "We're in the silliest situation I ever heard of. I've covered myself with ridicule for the rest of my days. I've been doing my utmost to track one brilliant fox, and my dog delivers me three of the creatures . . . with the intention that I take them home and bring them up, if I'm not mistaken. My reputation is mud."

He shrugged, and with laughter in his voice, asked the children, "What now? Are we to kill these infant terrors? Must we massacre them?"

The children protested noisily.

Tatie said, "Let's see, where do you suppose the mother and father of these cubs can be now?"

"They're certainly close by," said the Commandant, with a wave about the clearing. "They're waiting for us to make up our minds."

"Well, let's simply leave. The babies are safe and

comfortable where they are on the grass. If we go, their parents will come get them and put them back in the lair. We don't have to do anything about them at all."

"That's it," said the Commandant. "And then, next year, these adorable cubs will be around to dine on your chickens."

"You know what I think?" demanded Lina. "I don't think it can be so wonderful to be a chicken anyhow. If I had to choose for myself, I'd much rather be a fox."

"Me, too," said Piet.

He sounded so serious that everyone laughed.